the old lady who wrote stories for her son

P.R. HERNON

 FriesenPress

Suite 300 - 990 Fort St
Victoria, BC, V8V 3K2
Canada

www.friesenpress.com

Copyright © 2021 by P.R. Hernon
First Edition — 2021

ISBN
978-1-5255-9875-3 (Hardcover)
978-1-5255-9874-6 (Paperback)
978-1-5255-9876-0 (eBook)

1. FICTION, SHORT STORIES (SINGLE AUTHOR)

Distributed to the trade by The Ingram Book Company

TABLE OF CONTENTS

INTRODUCTION vii

OUR WRITING GROUP... ix

PART ONE {A STRANGE CIRCUMSTANCE} 1

THE FIND 3

PART TWO {MRS. LEWIS' FLASH STORIES} 9

THE PAINTING.. 11

ANSWERS... 13

CHINESE WHISPERS.. 15

SUMMER HAZE 17

WELL MAYBE 19

LIKE MINDS 21

A VENT INTO THE PSYCHE.. 23

THE WEIGHT OF CLOUDS 25

WHAT'S A PIZZA WITHOUT ANCHOVIES? 27

HIEROGLYPHICS.. 29

WILL IT EVER END?.. 31

CEREMONIAL DAY 33

THE GYPSY QUEEN 35

YET SO BEAUTIFUL.. 37

HERE WE GO AGAIN.. 39

WHO'S SORRY NOW? 41

THE JOURNEY... 43

THE PASSING OF BM 45

PARACHUTES AND FLOWERS.. 47

SONGBIRD 49

OLD WRINKLE PUSS 51

CASUALTY... 53

IF SEASONS WERE GENERATIONS.................................... 55

THE HOMILY 57

THE INTERLOPERS 59

THE DECISION...61

MISTAKEN IDENTITY 63

THE LITTLE VOICE 65

THE LASSO LOUNGE 67

A VOUCHER'S EXPIRATION 69

GIORGIO...71

EXIT 73

BEWARE OF SUGAR 75

A PERFECT TEMPLATE 77

A DOODLE 79

TICK TOCK..81

A FICKLE MASTER 83

PART THREE {MRS. LEWIS' SHORT STORIES} 85

DANCER..87

REVENGE OF THE COWS...91

THE SWEETHEART CRUISE..95

FRIENDS 99

THE BRIDGE..103

MYSTERY OF LADY TRIUMPH...109

THE WIGGLE ROOM..113

FIFTY DOLLARS WELL SPENT..119

THE LISTENING RAVENS...123

THE INTERVIEW..127

THE LAVENDER FIELD 131

I'LL TELL YOU TOMORROW..135

SOMETHING TO BELIEVE IN 139

THE GHOST CHAIR 143

PAPER FLOWERS FOR PAPA 147

TOO LATE..151

THE MAKINGS OF A HERO...155

CROSSED WIRES 159

ONCE, TWICE, AND GONE 163

MY HUSBAND..167

BIGMOUTH CANYON...171

A FARRAGO OF FACT AND MYTH 175

THE EMBODIMENT OF CAPITALISM 179
A POSITIVE OUTCOME 183
AN APOLOGY DOESN'T CUT IT 187
TALKING TO THE WIND 191
THE CONFESSIONAL 195
HOME FOR CHRISTMAS 201
PART FOUR {'TIS} **205**
'TIS 207
EPILOGUE 209

INTRODUCTION

Oh! Words …
Your bite and your caress
Your stab and your redress
Mediocre and sublime
Twisting and turning
In time … with the dance
Sometimes, perchance …
Communication

It is this communication that I have endeavoured to capture in the stories that follow. Words coax and cajole the imagination; they can tear down foundations of life and love but often build skyscrapers of understanding, meaning, and empathy from the rubble.

The words that I have used to fabricate my stories come from members of a writing group that I hosted for a number of years. As an exercise, at the end of every gathering, each of us would think randomly of a word to share with the members. The purpose for this was to stimulate the imagination, as we were then required to use these words in some form of writing that we would read aloud at the next meeting.

We were an eclectic group of five women and two men. Each of us was writing dissimilar pieces of work, ranging from self-help, poetry, memoir, creative non-fiction, and fiction. I used the words to inspire the flash and short stories you will find in this book.

This diverse group inspired wonderful, soul-searching discussions, critiques, and writings.

Although the valued members have gone their separate ways, I cherish the memory of laughter, tears, and personal disclosure that we shared in the safe environment of our writing group.

As a tribute, I share a poem I have written in remembrance of the writing group.

OUR WRITING GROUP

Together …
We travelled down the sunlit paths of memory
And the narrow alleyways of grief and loss.
We walked where secrets buried deep
Unmasked themselves in intimate disclosure.

Slumbering words awoke in joyous relief
And tumbling out, they coloured the welcoming page.
The endless churn of jubilant ideas came to life
To tint and spike the drowsing juice of imagination.

With fact and fantasy, tenacity and truth as weapons
We faced our fears and unravelled the scroll of life
And flung our hope and desperation
Upon the hotbed of creativity.

My stories reflect the many conundrums, enigmas, and puzzles of life.
They have dwelt in my imagination; now I splash them across the page and
leave them for you, the reader, to ponder.

PART ONE
{A STRANGE CIRCUMSTANCE}

THE FIND

The moving crew had removed the sparse furniture from the small fourth-floor apartment in the assisted living complex that morning.

Now two cleaners had come to dispose of any remaining articles and debris. They were surprised to find very little until one of them opened the small entryway closet.

"Hey, Jake, take a look at this," Gordon called out.

Jake came over to the open door and peered in. "What do we have here?"

They began hauling out two broken boxes filled with large manila envelopes and small white ones.

"Looks like letters. It may be important stuff. I'd better take a box of it down to the office and ask where they want it to go," Jake said.

"Okay, I'll start scrubbing the kitchen," Gordon replied.

As Jake walked down the hall to the elevator, a woman stopped him.

"Too bad about Mrs. Lewis. Maxine was a lovely woman. Lonely. She never had any visitors. Come to think of it, I don't either," she tittered nervously.

"She and I became good friends and now she's gone," she sighed.

"Sorry to hear that." Jake shook his head wondering how it must feel for someone to be neglected in a place like this. *Kind of a final stepping off into the unknown, alone,* he thought. A slight shiver ran through him.

The woman continued to speak as she followed Jake to the elevator. "What's your name?" she asked.

"I'm Jake. I'm cleaning Mrs. Lewis's apartment."

"Oh, I thought the movers cleared everything out yesterday."

"Almost, just a couple of boxes left."

As Jake stepped into the elevator, the elderly woman said, "I'm Elsa, Elsa Flowers."

"Nice to meet you," Jake replied, just as the elevator doors closed.

In the main office, Jake plunked the tattered box on the counter and called out, "Anybody here?"

"Yes, what is it?" A grey-haired woman arose from her desk behind the counter.

"I'm cleaning an apartment on the fourth floor, a Mrs. Lewis. We found two boxes of what looks like correspondence in the closet. Important stuff, I think. Maybe a relative should have it all," Jake said.

"No, no need to worry about it. That looks like the box that the group home sent to Mrs. Lewis after her son's death. Mrs. Lewis only had a son. He died a few months ago, no other relations."

Jake swayed back and forth. "I'm sorry to hear that. What a sad story."

"We have many sad stories here, but this is one of the most heartrending. Mrs. Lewis took care of her very physically handicapped son for most of his life. When she had to move into assisted living, he had to go into a group home. Now they are both gone. God bless them."

"So, what do I do? Just throw the boxes in the trash?"

"Yes, I'm afraid so. The bin is at the back of the building, as you may already know. Thank you for your consideration in asking about the boxes of mail. It has to go. Good day to you."

Jake walked slowly back to the elevator with the box tucked under his arm.

When he entered the apartment, he called out to Gordon, "Office says to junk it all. I'll take both boxes down to the trash bin now. Be right back."

It was a warm, sunny day and Jake wanted a smoke. He sat himself down on a small concrete wall behind the huge trash bins at the back of the parking lot. No one could see him from the building.

Jake plunked the boxes down at his feet. After a few drags on his cigarette, he absently picked up one of the manila envelopes. Inside he found a story with words written before the title. Inside another and another, more stories.

He opened one of the small white envelopes. Out tumbled little rectangular pieces of paper with a word written on each one. Inside another white envelope, more words, again and again, the same. There were five or six different words in each envelope.

Jake read one of the short stories and found that the words written at the top of the page were used in the story.

It dawned on him. *This is how mother and son kept in touch. Didn't the office lady say that Mrs. Lewis's son was physically disabled? But he still had a good intellect and a great sense of humour it seems. He sent words to his mom every few weeks. What a son! What a mom!*

"But why did they communicate this way?" Jake wondered.

Jake bent his head as tears blurred his vision. "I can't throw these stories away. Just wouldn't be right!" he said aloud.

"Once it's in the trash, it's common property," he mumbled to himself as he carried the damaged boxes to the cleaning van.

Don't know what I'll do with them. Just can't throw them in the trash. It'd be like disrespecting their memory – like stepping on their graves or something...

When Jake entered the apartment, Gordon yelled, "What took you so long, Jake? It's quitting-time. I'm finished here, but you still have to clean the carpets."

"Okay, Gordon, go on home now. I'll finish up here. See you Monday. We have another apartment to clean on this floor. Have a good weekend."

An hour later, Jake stood still in the now empty apartment and murmured, "Guess I'm finished here."

Jake hauled out the cleaning supplies to the cart in the hallway. At the elevator, Jake suddenly turned away and walked back to the apartment. He opened the door and stood looking around the empty room. Tears filled his eyes. He quickly wiped them away with his calloused hand.

This can't be all there is, he thought.

He clenched his fist and sniffed back more tears, "No, Mrs. Lewis and son, you may have moved on, but you won't be forgotten. I'll be doing some reading tonight for sure. Got to get to the bottom of this whole thing."

Later that night, Jake sat sorting the envelopes into piles, manila envelopes in one pile, white envelopes in another. All were sorted according to the date of the postal stamp.

He was still pondering why a mother and son would communicate this way. Couldn't they just phone each other?

Monday morning, Jake arrived early on the fourth floor. As he was moving the cart and supplies off the elevator, he heard someone say, "Oh, good morning, Jake. You're here early."

"Oh, hi Elsa. It is Elsa, isn't it?"

"Yes, that's me, Elsa Flowers. You are cleaning 408, I suppose. Mr. Douglas, such a nice man. Two gone in a week. So sad. Would you like to come in for a coffee? It's too early to start working, and your helper isn't here yet."

Jake could sense that Elsa had something on her mind.

"Okay, I'll just put the cart into Number 408."

Elsa followed Jake down the hall and waited for him in the hallway. When he came out of the apartment, she tucked her arm through his and led him to her door.

"Sit down here at the table. You'll love this coffee, Jake. I still use my mother's old percolator coffee pot," she said, as she placed the steaming mug before Jake.

"Cream and sugar, Jake?"

"No thanks. I take it black."

Jake looked over at Elsa as she sat across from him. She was fidgeting with a ring on her finger. Round and round, she twisted it. It was making Jake nervous. Finally, Jake could stand it no more. He blurted, "Elsa, seems like you got something on your mind. Out with it."

"Mmm, maybe you'll think I'm a nosey old woman, but okay, here goes."

Elsa's eyes filled with tears. She took a deep breath and blurted out, "I need to know. What was in the boxes you threw into the trash on Friday?"

Jake was stunned at the question. He stammered, "Some envelopes filled with words and stories. Why are you asking?"

"Oh, do you think we could go down to the trash and rescue them?"

"Really, no need to do that. I kept them," he said sheepishly.

"Oh! Thank God!" Elsa squealed. She jumped up and kissed Jake on his cheek.

"Once in the trash, it's common property, you know. I'm going to read every one of them. Did Mrs. Lewis share the stories with you?"

"Oh no, that was one thing she would not do. I would have loved to read them. Now, of course I can't, even if I wanted to. My eyesight has diminished; glaucoma, they call it. Maxine hoarded the words and stories to herself. I guess she needed to have that one last bond with her son. He was amazing. When he was only twenty-two, he was in a terrible car accident that left him a paraplegic. She looked after him all those years. After Mrs. Lewis took ill, she had to come here, and her son had to go into a group home.

"Yeah, I heard that, but my question is: Why did they communicate this way? Couldn't they just visit or phone each other?"

"Oh, they talked to each other every week and even visited once in a while until six months ago, when both of them declined in health. Maxine's son was a real joker. He was very solicitous of his mom. He sent words to her and challenged her to write stories using the words. He tried to keep her mind active."

"Well, she sure accepted the challenge. Say, Elsa, how about I read some of the stories to you? I could come over once a week for a cup of your special coffee. Are you doing anything this Sunday afternoon?"

"Me, doing anything? Besides being bored out of my mind? No! Would you really visit every week, Jake?" Elsa was trembling and tears were popping out of her eyes.

"Here's what we'll do. I'll come on Sundays and read you a story in exchange for a cup of your excellent coffee. Is it a deal Elsa?"

"A cup of my excellent coffee for a story every Sunday afternoon? It's a deal, young man!"

"One more thing, Elsa. Where I come from, a deal has to be cemented with a hug."

PART TWO
{MRS. LEWIS' FLASH STORIES}

*Abstract *Bushwhacker *Time
*Blue *Platform

THE PAINTING

The art gallery's platform was to stage their paintings in such a way as to encourage enlightened comment and even friendly banter. But … this time it went too far.

The ambience upon arrival was soothing. A piano was playing the silky blues of Etta James, and the lighting was subdued. The seniors group strolled through the wide, curved aisle and spoke in hushed tones as the paintings inspired reflection and almost a spiritual awe. Pastoral scenes of slave bushwhackers, backs bent clearing woods, and women bent down picking and stacking the cut vegetation were placed at strategic points to draw the eye and stimulate the psyche.

It wasn't until the curved aisle widened to reveal a huge abstract painting, which took up the entire twenty-foot wall and blasted the sensibilities of the patrons, that the animated discussions began.

"Anyone can see that the painting depicts Armageddon. Look at the blood falling from the sky!" observed one old woman.

A man retorted, "Some imagination you have, lady. It is nothing of the sort! Can't you see the image of a race horse?"

"It is just a blob of confusion," said another little old woman thumping her cane for emphasis.

"You are all nuts!" a white-haired, wrinkled-faced man yelled. "It is just somebody's idea of a joke."

"A joke? This painting could be worth half a million, you uneducated fool!" snapped a well-dressed lady as she pushed her walker over the man's foot.

"Ow! What did you do that for?" he hollered.

Bedlam ensued as the others in the group raised their voices.

"Who is she calling uneducated?" roared an offended person.

"Uppity bitch," yelled another.

It took three security guards and the two tour guides to escort the group out of the venue.

All was once again circumspect and silent, as it should be in the hallowed space of an art gallery, when a man pushing his six-year-old son in a wheelchair stopped in front of the pulsing, multi-coloured, gigantic abstract painting.

The little boy's eyes widened and he cried out, "Papa, look! It's the world! See, mother earth is smiling!"

Then the boy asked, "What is the name of the painting?"

The father looked over at the gold-rimmed plaque and replied, "The artist has named his painting, '*Tis*."

"What does '*Tis*' mean, Papa?"

The father gazed down at his son and said quietly, "'*Tis*' means 'it is'"

> And so it is ... and was ...
> And will forever be ...
> Life's canvas reflects
> Back to self
> The who and what
> We see.

*Computer *Truth *Remember
*Meditation *Entice

ANSWERS

The day I discovered that Papa did not have all the answers was a great shock to me. Up to this point I could ask him anything. "How high is up? Why is the sky blue? How many sleeps till Santa comes? How many inches in a foot? Where do babies come from?" He would always have an answer.

But today … not today. He just looked at me in silence. Finally he muttered, "Sonny, you're a young man now. You're eighteen; find your own answers. Don't always ask someone else. Do the work yourself."

"Papa, I only asked you if I should buy a computer."

"Sorry, Sonny, you're on your own. You earned the money, now you decide." He turned back to his pipe and newspaper.

I was stunned. I felt betrayed. How could he do this to me? I had never felt so alone, except for the day my dog, Samson, died. I walked out of the house and sat brooding on the front step.

As I sat, thoughts began racing through my mind. Hadn't my friend, Louisa said almost the same thing to me? Yeah, just last week she told me I was too dependent upon others. I remember defending myself. "You don't know me!"

"You don't know yourself," she said, as she walked away.

Now it got me to wondering if maybe there was a truth here somewhere. First Louisa and now Papa.

Weeks went by. I avoided Louisa and only said mild things to Papa, nothing that would stir up pepper-hot comments. I was still in pondering mode.

Then, one day, I went to the library and right there in front of me was a table with a big poster propped up on it. In big red letters it said:

FIND THE ANSWERS – KNOW YOURSELF – MEDITATION – RELAXATION CLASSES – ONE-DAY WORKSHOP - $50.00

It sounded so enticing, so I signed up right away, paid the fee, and felt very proud of my decision-making ability. And … I hadn't asked anyone.

The lady at the table assured me that I would really enjoy the workshop. She said, "You will find your Spiritual Guide."

"Whoa!" I thought. Wait a minute!" But it was too late. I had already paid my fifty dollars.

That workshop changed my life. Over the years, I graduated with a PhD in psychology, earned a fellowship in Mid-Eastern philosophy, and married Louisa. We have two grown children, a son and daughter.

Yesterday my daughter asked me if she should use her babysitting money to buy her grad dress or save it for a trip to Italy.

I found myself saying, "Greta, you're eighteen now. Find your own answers. Don't always ask someone else. Do the work yourself."

She hasn't talked to me for a few days. She is still pondering. I don't mind. She will make her way. I know the drill.

This morning I visited Papa at the nursing home. He was glad to see me and held on to me when I bent to hug him.

"How are you doing, Papa? They treating you well?"

"Okay, okay, doing fine." He picked at his tie. "Only thing is, Sonny, I don't know if I should have the steak and kidney pie or the spaghetti with meat sauce for supper. What do you think?"

"Oh, Papa."

Chemist *Light* *Nimble* *Taunting*
Telephone *Enrolled* *Legacy*

CHINESE WHISPERS

It was just after the Second World War that my father, a chemist, was hired by the Canadian Government to do research for them. We were British. We left England in tatters and came to this small community near the city of Lethbridge, Alberta, where the Old Man River ran undisturbed and people seemed quaint, fit, and healthy. It was a great treat to see.

Now when I look back, I realize that it was not the legacy of the fact that my father was a chemist that put me in bad stead with the fifth-grade class my mother had enrolled me in. It was my British accent, vocabulary, and so-called uppity ways that seemed to annoy my classmates. The taunting began immediately, so I had to be light of foot and nimble-minded to escape the traps my fellow students set for me. I really did not mind it at all. In fact, I found it fascinating, especially when I could devise ways to gain a subtle upper hand.

It all came to a head at the birthday party of Eric Lin. I had accepted the invitation at the insistence of my mother. "You will never make friends if you are snobbish," she said.

All went well until someone asked if anyone knew a good game to play. I piped up, "I know of a peachy game. It is called Chinese Whispers."

Well, this unsettled Eric Lin. "What do you know about Chinese anything? Are you trying to be a racist?"

All the others joined in and slammed me for my words.

Daniel Frome said, "Let's play Telephone."

It was my turn to be obtuse. "What kind of a game is Telephone for heaven's sake? It sounds mundane."

Then Rosie O'Donnell said, "Let's play Gossip then."

We all were silent because no one knew what this game was either. So one by one each of the three of us explained what our game was about.

I started and said, "Chinese Whispers is a game where we sit in a circle and someone whispers a sentence into the ear of the person next to him. Then that person whispers what he heard into the ear of the person next to him. This goes on until the last person says aloud what he has heard."

Daniel and Rosie burst out laughing, "They are all the same game, just different titles."

Everyone joined in the laughter. I then explained that the name Chinese Whispers was because we Brits thought so highly of the Chinese writing system. We could not decipher it, so the Chinese were more intelligent.

Eric Lin nodded and said in a loud voice, "Yes, of course we are!"

Paul Robillard said, "Now let's just play, okay? Let Potter, our Brit, start it off."

I did and minutes later, Donna Benson, the last person to hear the whisper, stood up to speak.

"Okay, Donna. What did you hear?" Eric prompted.

Donna blushed red as a beet. She said, "I'd like to be in Newfoundland with frogs!"

"Now Potter has to say what he said at the beginning," Eric Lin said.

"Righto! Here is what I said. I certainly like my newfound friends."

Laughter rocked the room! We all became good friends after that party. We began sharing our experiences of wartime in Canada and England. We were, after all, in a strange way, compatriots.

*Fried*Stand*Harbour
*Agreement*Community

SUMMER HAZE

The smoky haze from forest fires hangs from the gallows of the sky like a sullen ghost today. As if in some unspoken agreement, the earth has collaborated with the firmament to create a masterpiece of portending doom.

An eerie fog clings to the trees and drapes its pernicious grey shroud over the city, the harbour, and the distant hills. The raucous calls of seagulls and crows seem softened as the pall mutes their voices.

The entire animal community, including humans, is affected in some way or another. Humans cough and sneeze, dogs pant, bees lie helpless in the hearts of flowers; all seeking shelter from the noxious, murky gloom.

A filter of morning light furtively peeks through the suspended particles of burnt tree ash embedded in the atmosphere. The sun boldly tries to break out but is impeded by the thick layer. It is suspended like a burning red orb hanging helplessly in what was once a blue morning sky.

Perhaps this is a different kind of mourning – a requiem for hectares of flash-fried, burnt forests; forty percent of which were caused by man's recklessness. There the trees stand, the giants of Mother Nature, like blackened skeletons, their feet buried in grey funereal ash, weeping for the animals and life they had sustained and protected, now incinerated.

I ask … where is their protection? Is this a foreshadowing of times to come? Wherein the earth says, "Basta! Enough! It is time…" And a wrathful blood moon looks down to witness the earth's baptism by fire.

*Roses *Mother *Shirt
*Talk *Wail

WELL MAYBE

I'll never talk to that SOB again! Not even if he sends ten dozen roses delivered by Adonis himself; not even if he apologizes on his knees in front of my mother; not even if he cries and wails and rips his shirt off ...

Well maybe ... if he rips his shirt off ...

*Duck *Sympathy *Volatile
*Petulant *Savour *Kumquat

LIKE MINDS

Everyone ducked behind anything available when they saw Julie coming. No one had sympathy for her. *Why should they?* was their thought. Overnight she had changed into a loony, they said. One moment she was all soft and gracious; the next a screaming meemie.

Yes, she was beautiful, but her petulance and often volatile explosions of insults wore on all of her onetime friends like a slow, grinding, zigzag torture.

No one bothered to understand what was happening to their once pleasant friend.

One day, she flared off in a restaurant, where she overturned a dish of savoury curry, screeching that the cooks had tried to poison her.

Police were called. She was taken to a psychiatric facility, where she was diagnosed with bi-polar disorder. Months later, she was released and tried to go back to her life, but she remembered how her friends had distained her, so she avoided them. She became as lonely and isolated as a desert mesa.

Months later, Julie had a chance encounter with a sympathetic woman in Starbucks, where she had stopped for a chocolate latte. The woman told her that she was a writer, and after hearing Julie's story, she invited her to join the group of writers.

"I'd like that. What's the name of your group?" Julie asked.

"Oh, we've been trying to come up with a good name, but so far no luck."

When the group heard of the treatment Julie had endured she was encouraged to write her story of triumph.

Another of the writers said, "Your friends are nothing but fools with not even the brains of a kumquat."

Loud laughter followed. Then one man slammed his hand on the table, "That's it!"

"What's it?" they all chimed.

"Our group name!" he replied.

"The Kumquats! The sweet and the acid, just like what a true writer feels and writes about."

They all nodded in agreement.

*Butterflies *Pallid *Question
*Sadly *Trance *Vent

A VENT INTO THE PSYCHE

He seemed an utterly pallid and charmless character at first glance. He was whey-faced with wild eyes the colour of slate and clothes to match.

I met him at the edge of the forest walkway, and to tell the truth, I was scared to death. I thought he was a fugitive from an asylum or worse a druggie. He stood aside to let me pass, and as he did so, he mumbled, "Nice day to see 'em ma'am."

As his shoulder brushed mine I felt something strange, like an electric zap. It stopped me in my tracks. I turned to face him. Our eyes met. I was flooded with shame for what I had thought of him for his smile illuminated my soul.

Trancelike I asked, "See what, sir?"

"The butterflies. There's a kaleidoscope near that tree right there."

I looked to my right and was amazed to see hundreds of butterflies of all colours floating in the air. He put out his arm and some landed on it. Others flew around his head like a halo. He reached out to me, and the butterflies swirled around me too in a glorious cloud of colour. I stood mesmerized. Time seemed to halt.

Sadly, it all ended when a group of children ran by shouting and laughing.

I turned to thank this gracious man, whom I had misjudged so unfairly, but he was gone.

To this day I question myself. Was he really there? Was he a figment of my imagination? Whatever this was, I knew that I had had a vision into the depths of my soul.

I have since walked that forest path, but never again did I see that wondrous man and the butterflies. Now I see the wonder and beauty of the butterflies in all people I meet.

*Fussy *Timeless *Candy
*Brilliant *Cloud *Street

THE WEIGHT OF CLOUDS

In the beginning, the townspeople of Antrodoco, Italy called him Brilianto because he seemed to have an answer to every question they asked him. He would often be stopped in the middle of the cobbled sidewalk by some inquiring soul asking puzzling questions, such as: "Why won't pigs eat cucumbers?" or "Why does a dog circle many times before lying down?"

He always gave a piece of candy to a child who asked a question because he believed questions were the basis of education and discovery. He knew that questions were timeless. "Mankind has always striven for truth and answers," he would say to anyone who was the least bit interested.

Brilianto was fastidious in his attire and very fussy about what he ate. Although he loved bananas, he would often dispose of an entire banana or a grape if there was even a hint of a bruise on the outer skin. He was a good man and kind, content with his idiosyncrasies and competence.

He was not vain nor unctuous, never ingratiating himself to appear more than what and who he believed himself to be. He accepted the name of Brilianto because he knew what he knew he knew.

What he did not know is that there will always be a question that has yet to be asked and an answer that has yet to be discovered.

This was the day his world changed.

A young boy came to him that morning as Brilianto was in the barn milking a cow.

"Good morning, Brilianto," the boy chirped. "I've been lying out there in the meadow looking up at the sky and wondering about something."

"What is it that has got you wondering?" Brilianto asked.

"Well, it's a funny question, but I know you can give me the answer, so here goes: How much do clouds weigh?"

Brilianto was silent for a moment, and then he jumped up, knocked the milk pail over, and holding his head in his hands, shouted at the boy, "*Dio mio, Dio mio*, Oh, my God, I don't know!" Tears cascaded down his face.

The boy ran off in terror.

The years wore on. The townsfolk now called Brilianto, "Matto", which translates as "Loony"!

Loony no longer welcomed anyone to his farm. He no longer walked on the cobbled streets of the town. Nor did he ever recover from what he assumed was self-inflicted ignorance. He died an ignoble death centuries before this question could be answered.

Never knowing that liquid water content = 1 gram per cubic metre. Never knowing that the weight of a thunderstorm cloud is 1.7 billion pounds.

*Anchovies *Acid *Admonish
*Silence *Archaic *Smile

WHAT'S A PIZZA
WITHOUT ANCHOVIES?

"What's a pizza without anchovies?" the old man hollered. "You mean you don't have anchovies in this pizza parlour? *Dio mio!* And you advertise Italian food? You are a fraud!"

"Calm down, Pops," said a young man sitting at a nearby table. "You'll have a heart attack. Try the pizza with feta and spinach. It's really good. Sometimes we have to leave our archaic mindsets behind and explore new horizons; don't you agree, Pops?"

The old man was stunned into silence, his angst forgotten. A friendly young man was actually talking to him! This had never happened before. He looked at the young man and was surprised to see the wide smile turned on him even though he had been admonished.

"Come on over and sit with me, Pops," the fellow said.

The old man stumbled to his feet and went to sit with the young man who had already pulled out a chair for him.

The young man signalled the waiter and ordered two Greek pizzas and two beers.

The old man hesitated and then said, "I don't have enough for a pizza and a beer. I'll just have the pizza."

"No way, Pops, the treat is on me," the altruistic young man said.

Tears sprang to the old man's eyes, and he said, "Many thanks, young fella, many thanks."

The pizzas came, the beer came, and as the pair munched and sipped a strange repartee developed and there was much teasing and joking.

When they parted two hours later, the old man had even forgotten to mention his acid reflux condition to the young man. Instead, that night as he burped and regurgitated, he thought that it was quite a change and relief to not have the rancid taste of anchovies in his mouth.

Maybe these young ones really do know something, he thought as he shook his head and smiled.

*Telephone poles *Hieroglyphics *Melodious
*Sulphuric *Palpable *Poignant

HIEROGLYPHICS

The silence is palpable, a living thing holding its breath as the last melodious note from the throat of the trumpet floats away into the frosty air. The crack of rifle fire bursts the moment. Then the hush settles again, weighing heavy on all the mourners.

Eyes closed I stand on the grass a little back from the family, the collar of my coat hiding my unshaven, distraught face. I do not have to add to their grief.

Suddenly a child's voice calls, "Daddy, don't go!"

Whispered voices, comforting, sobbing quietly. Another child's voice, "Don't cry, Tommy. Daddy's gone to heaven. He's with the angels now."

"I don't want him in heaven! I want him here right now," the little boy yells. He screams and stamps his feet and then collapses in tears.

The distraught mother picks him up, turns abruptly away from the flower-draped casket, and says, "Let's all go home now."

The finality of it all, the indescribable feeling of hopelessness, the sadness dripping from the air and even from the willow trees, which hover over the lawns, overwhelms me. I too turn away and head home. There is nothing more here for anyone. But, this poignant moment will haunt me forever.

As I drive the highway back to my house, I see telephone poles seemingly standing at attention, lined up like soldiers on parade honouring my friend, that brave, stupid son of a gun, who thought he could beat the odds in Afghanistan. I pound the steering wheel.

My mouth feels hot. My face is on fire. I realize he is gone, my friend of thirty years. The memories crowd in: Boys playing street hockey, fighting over the hottie Nancy Groth in high school, stuffing ourselves with pizza and beer, shouting at the touchdown. Too many. Overload.

Tears come, sulphuric, bitter, helpless. I pull off onto a country road. I sit behind the wheel, wailing like a banshee. Finally, the sobs stop.

I know his death will never be understood by me, never validated. And my grief, I know too, will always be there, undecipherable as ancient hieroglyphics.

*Willow *Moth *Popcorn
*Morning *Sympathy

WILL IT EVER END?

The glider aircraft flew low over the woods, where the willows grow, almost as if it were a giant, white moth. The stream of bubbling and gurgling water reflected the blue sky above. In the distance, the pealing of church bells could be heard.

Suddenly, the harmony of the morning was shattered. A peppering of gunshots, sounding to the untrained ear like popcorn popping to the nth degree. This startled the crows. Their raucous calls vibrated throughout the forest, causing a quake of fear wherein even the trees quivered.

On the path leading to the edge of the woods a man lay facedown, trembling. Beside him a golden retriever sat with his paw over the man's head.

As minutes went by, the man stilled and slowly arose. "Thanks, old chum. I guess it was just a hunter shooting grouse," he said, as he patted the dog's head.

Later that day, at the veterans' meeting, he told of his morning's trauma. "Will it ever end?" he asked shakily. Others nodded in sympathy and the meeting went on.

*Pedagogue *Howl *Slapstick
*Striped socks *Rattan *Anger

CEREMONIAL DAY

The dilapidated rattan chair on which the plump posterior of the headmaster rested creaked loudly.

"Did you say something, sir?" a younger teacher asked.

"What? No. Why do you ask?" the headmaster answered as the rattan chair groaned again under its burden.

When the young teacher realized what the sound was, he began to grin and could hardly keep from laughing aloud as once again the chair complained.

Suddenly the pedagogue did speak, in ringing tones. "Is nothing sacred?" he said to the younger man.

They were watching the school's religious procession passing by. It was led by an angelic-looking young man, seemingly sober and reverently clad in the dark sombre robes befitting the ceremonial parade. Fifty young students followed their leader.

The teacher turned to the headmaster and saw the glint of righteous anger and the flushed face of his superior. "What do you refer to, sir?"

"Look! Can't you see the young whippersnapper has his pants rolled up, and he's not wearing shoes! Oh, Lord, he is wearing black and red striped socks! He is in for trouble, I tell you."

"I hope nobody else sees this," the younger man said.

"I only pray the Bishop does not notice the lapse in holy protocol. This is not a slapstick comedy!" the headmaster said. He surveyed the crowd, hoping to see if anyone else had noticed the transgression.

People were lined up on either side of the street. As the procession passed, a ripple of something as stealthy and silent as a cougar stalking its prey began to manifest. Grins, then wide smiles began to light the faces of the onlookers as the boys marched past.

The headmaster looked again at the passing parade. All of the boys had their pant legs rolled up, and there he saw that each of them were shoeless and wore striped socks: yellow and orange, blue and white, purple and green, and red and indigo. The boys also all had solemn, placid faces of devoutness.

The headmaster gasped, the rattan chair whimpered, and the crowd finally could not contain its mirth. Loud, boisterous howls of laughter erupted as boy after boy passed.

The rattan chair gave a sharp death rattle and down went the headmaster in a heap, broken bits of rattan imbedded in his robes. The young teacher hauled the headmaster up, but made quite a mess of it as he too was roaring with contagious laughter.

Once on his feet, the headmaster dared not glance at the platform across the way wherein the Bishop sat. He knew he would be censured and held to account for this shocking display of disrespect later that day when he would meet the Bishop for lunch.

However, if he had looked to where the Bishop sat, he would have seen a remarkable sight. The Bishop had his feet on the railing and his pants rolled up to the knees. On his shoeless feet were red and white striped socks.

Even Bishops sometimes tire of ritual and propriety. If anyone dared to ask him why he had arranged this departure from convention, he would simply have quoted Douglas Jerrold, "O, glorious laughter! Thou man-loving spirit, that for a time doth take the burden from the weary back, that doth lay salve to the weary feet..."

*Frumpy *Fishpond *Friendship
*Reward *Allow *Barquentine

THE GYPSY QUEEN

"Okay, so I'm fat. Is that any reason to call me frumpy?" My eyes peer into those of my accuser, and I know that our friendship cum-relationship is teetering on the brink of collapse.

"I'm just saying that you can't come with me to the gallery looking like *that*. This is a posh affair, and there you are in some gaudy sack of a dress. I'm amazed that you think I would be seen with you looking like this."

I gulp back tears as the lecture goes on.

"You know I have worked on this project for over two years, constructing that intricate barquentine inside that massive jug with the small opening. Tonight will be my reward for all my work. I intend to come away with first prize. I simply won't allow you to ruin my chances by accompanying me looking like a gypsy."

Something gives way inside of me, but instead of the usual flood of tears, a rage as red hot as a slave's branding iron explodes out of me like a volcano. I spit out years of castigation, shouting like a fishwife, "You bastard! How dare you speak to me like this? I have lived with you for ten years like a bloody lackey. I have been swimming in your stagnant fishpond, hoping for a crumb of acceptance, a measure of humanity. No more!"

I run over to the display shelf where the glass bottle shines and the beautiful ship within it sails on a sea of blue paper waves. I pick it up, hold it high over my head, and screech like a night owl.

The edict of shattered glass. No other sound. The silence of shock.

I look down and see the ship, all sails intact, seemingly floating on a sea of gleaming glass. It has escaped its crystal confinement.

I know with a certainty that I cannot do less.

I glance over to where he stands, mouth wide open, speechless. Without a word, I turn and walk out of the room, wide hips swinging, double chins held high.

The gypsy queen.

*Strumpet *Pontificate *Lasciviousness
*Challenge *Brouhaha *Whispered

YET SO BEAUTIFUL

"I ask you," the lawyer for the defence said as his final statement to the jury, "would this woman be here if it were not for the lasciviousness of men?"

The lawyer for the prosecution glared at the defence lawyer but did not make a move to reply. He had already given his pontificated address to the jury, citing the obvious guilt of the defendant. "A strumpet, a prostitute, the worst of all womankind." He had almost snarled the words. They dripped from his lips in self-righteous anger and disgust. "She viciously murdered the man. That is all there is to it! There can be no challenge. She is guilty!" This was his final plea to the twelve jury members, eleven of whom were men.

The judge's gavel rapped again and again as whispered protests were heard throughout the gallery, where one hundred women onlookers sat to view the proceedings.

"I will have silence in this courtroom or you will all be escorted out," he growled in a voice that held grave authority. "The jury will now deliberate."

The verdict came back within the hour. "Guilty!" the jury foreman announced. The lone woman on the jury hung her head and could not look at the defendant.

The death sentence was carried out within the year, after retrial and protests.

When her mother visited the gravesite, she kissed a framed photo of the so-called strumpet that had been set into the gravestone. In the photograph, the girl was smiling and waving, her young face an image of innocence.

After the brouhaha had settled, a newspaper editorial page printed this poem written by "anonymous" and sent from the county prison weeks before.

TRAPPED

What do you do when your father
Does unfatherly things to you?
Do you stay and watch as sisters
Fall under his evil spell too?

I had to escape – I had to
But then where could I go?
I went to the mall at midnight
And that's when I met Joe

I thought my life would be better
His promised protection believed
Then reality entered the picture
I was once again deceived.

I'm what is called a hooker
And sure as hell I'm hooked
I have no rest or solace
For every night I'm booked

For this guy or that or another
There is for me no choice
Just as it was with my father
I had no voice.

anonymous

*Stone-faced *Cycling *Blank
*Pile *Worms *Sunny

HERE WE GO AGAIN

It was not the first time I saw it happen, this "love at first sight" thing.

There they were, sitting across from each other at the poker table. He is stone-faced with a huge pile of poker chips in front of him; she, deadpan blank. The magnetism was palpable, cycling energy between them like a whirling dervish. Both, trying so hard to keep their minds focused on the game.

I watch in fascination. The lure is cast.

He dumps his pile of chips into the middle of the table as he stares directly into her green eyes.

She folds, putting her cards face down, closes her eyes, dark eyelashes caressing her face. She sighs, bosom rising and falling as she worms her way into his psyche. Looks up … a sunny smile.

Integration complete.

*Tickle *Astonishing *Sunscreen *Star

WHO'S SORRY NOW?

It tickles me to see Eva Stratton talking to herself as she puts bags of cat food in her grocery cart. The astonishing fact is that, even though she had not been negligent in using sunscreen during those tortured years of youth, she still looks as wrinkled as an old, used Kleenex. She used to think of herself as a movie star, dressing in the latest fashions that put us all to shame and putting on airs as if she were not from the same midtown dump where we all lived.

I'm home from Toronto for my father's funeral and surely never expected to see her still here in Nowheresville.

I am behind her in the grocery line. "I'm sorry, Eva, but you are three dollars short," the clerk is saying.

Eva looks down and digs into her crumpled bag, pulling out debris and mumbling an apology. She is shaking and tears are pouring down her face. She turns and looks directly at me, not a drop of recognition in her eyes.

Now, I'm the big shot. I say, "Here, let me make up the difference." I hand the clerk three dollars and feel like I have really done my good deed for the day.

Eva mumbles a thank you and shakily pushes her cart out the door.

I look at the clerk and raise my eyebrows in derision.

The clerk ignores my superior stance and says, "That was kind of you. That woman is a saint. She has had MS ever since she turned eighteen, but she still works at the Animal Rescue Shelter every day."

I slink out of the store and wonder into which part of hell my humanity has fled.

*Sunspots *Sunflower seeds *Wisteria
*Harmony *Potassium

THE JOURNEY

Ma has left, her words hanging like purple wisteria in springtime. I can almost smell them. Kind, tender murmurs falling like gentle mist, "You will soon be home, Sonny. I love you."

I know I don't have much time left. The stay hasn't happened. Only two hours to go and then it's finished.

I had to laugh at the look on their faces when I ordered salted sunflower seeds and a Coke for my last meal.

Said no to the clergyman. I've made my peace, done my time, ready for what comes next. Doc says the potassium chloride solution is quick; a prick of the needle then it's over.

Lying here looking up at the grey ceiling, wishing there was some colour, just a little blue; maybe some yellow and green would be nice, but no … grey, stone grey, like an undertaker's gloves. Guess I don't deserve colour. I can handle that.

Footsteps coming for me … I know the drill.

Strapping me down …

"No, I've nothing to say, just get it over with. No one thinks I'm innocent anyhow, a sorry won't change anything."

My eyes wide open behind the black hood.

A prick, the needle …

I'm walking the last leg of a journey it seems. I hear a harmony of bird song like a concerto. I feel warmth, the sun! Oh! The sun! I see a stream of cool water meandering crookedly between fields of flowers and a mountain running away from me …

The sun … black sunspots on the sun … polka dots dancing on the sun … getting bigger and bigger … blotting out the sun …

Pitch-blackness … black sludge sucking me into it …

Voiceless calling, "Help me, Mama!"

Reaching up! Reaching up!

A pinpoint of light, brighter than the sun … expanding … opening … opening …

*Pulse *Whisper *Blabbermouth
*Story *True

THE PASSING OF BM

Some people just can't help it, I guess. They are who they are. Take Jeremiah Jenkins for example. He is vertically challenged in stature but long on words. He is the town's blabbermouth, known as BM (tongue-in-cheek) for short. If you want to know anything about anyone or anything, he is there spouting off non-stop, a geyser of gossip, tittle–tattle, rumour, and strangely enough, often factual information laced with witticisms and deep ponderings. Some call his rhetoric fulsome and exaggerated. Others call him a prophet.

And sure enough, didn't he predict that Oscar Brownwood would win the mayoral race in our town and that there would be an attack in America leading to the collapse of the towers in New York City … after which, he said triumphantly, "I have my fingers on the pulse of the world."

Although BM is often resented and tolerated, he is also respected. However, there is not a whisper of humbleness in the man. And … herein lay his downfall.

For don't you know that even the mighty are not immune to life's payback for arrogance? Well, the story goes like this.

BM ran greyhounds, and he had a prize-winner in Stretcher. This dog was a marvel of swift, suave motion. Over the past three years, he had made BM a small fortune. This May, the race had drawn international attention. The shopkeepers were jubilant, the two hotels were fully booked, TV crews had arrived, and the townsfolk were excited.

Those who believed that BM was a prophet bet heavily on Stretcher. After all, hadn't BM foretold a win, a high-stake surety? Even those who half-believed the probabilistic measurement of winning that BM espoused took a chance on Stretcher. BM himself laid his small fortune on the betting counter, smug in his sure knowledge of a big payoff.

Well, true to the age-old adage that "pride goeth before a fall," disaster struck. Just as poor Stretcher had stretched one race too far, coming in fourth, BM too had over-stretched his prophetic powers. Devastation!

One can only imagine the chagrin of the townspeople who had bet all their savings on the race. BM was ostracized and publicly shamed as he slunk away.

The last I heard, he and Stretcher now live in a rundown cabin in Kelly Woods just half a mile from the racetrack. BM is sometimes seen after midnight roaming around the enclosure, picking up empty beer cans and pop bottles and loading them onto Stretcher's backpack as he prognosticates loudly to the moon.

*Radiant *Perspective *Symbiotic
*Seaweed *Sometimes

PARACHUTES AND FLOWERS

I doodle rectangular boxes now – coffins I suppose. I used to doodle parachutes and flowers. That was before the doctor told me I have only three months left to live. What do you do with news like that?

Time, like long, green strands of seaweed, twists around my days. My waking hours are bound with memories of him. They slip and slide over the same hills of hurt and barren regions of regret. My dreams, if I manage to sleep, are replicas of my days.

I wasn't much of a father. Always away on one mission or another, trying to save the world, not understanding that my son should have been my main focus and to hell with all the medals and accolades I earned from the Special Forces. I failed at the greatest mission of my life, my family.

I phoned him yesterday and told him all this, but I haven't heard back. Did I really expect to?

How long before I can put all this into perspective, any semblance of order? I have faced death many times. I have the scars to prove it, but this is different. I am trapped in the past, but it is my present that I have to come to grips with.

Guess I'll just haul my worthless ass over to the sofa, release my prosthesis, open a can of Molson, light up a toke, and hope the pain goes away.

You know how sometimes you know you are dreaming, but you don't want to wake up? Well, there I am floating down from a great height, dangling from a huge, white parachute. The sun is radiant, white clouds drifting by on a sky-like blue indigo. This time I'm not tense with adrenaline surfing through me like an electric charge. There is no gunfire, no smoke billowing up from some target hit on the ground. Only the gentle swaying of a breeze, rocking me like I'm in my mother's arms … There is a chiming of bells.

I awake with a start. The doorbell chimes again. I hobble over to the door on one leg, holding onto the wall and furniture. No one has been around for three weeks. Now it's another do-gooder from the Legion, I suppose, here to brace me up.

I release the dead bolt and peer into the face of the intruder.

"Oh my God, Jessie, is it really you?" I grasp onto my son, and he doesn't pull away. Instead, he hugs me back and kisses me.

"Hi, Pop, how's it going?"

I am shaking so bad that I can't speak. Tears are cascading down our faces.

"Pop, I would have been here sooner had I known," he croaks. "Nothing could keep me away, you know that don't you?"

I didn't know that. And the realization hits me like a mortar. The symbiotic relationship between a son and his father is unbreakable and, in this case, undeserved.

But … there it is.

*Vanilla *Commit *Egg *Star

SONGBIRD

Yes, she was beautiful with her vanilla-coloured dark hair, and yes, she did sing like a songbird. In fact, that is what they called her all those years ago in high school, Songbird. She was like the bird known as the Common Cowbird – beautiful to behold but always laying her eggs in other people's nests.

She was my sister, but back then, I had often wished she wasn't. I was always cleaning up her messes – making peace with those she offended, calming the gossip she initiated, taking the rap for her when Pop's cigarettes and booze went missing.

It was a real struggle for me, especially fighting off her admirers. Here I was, a five foot six, skinny guy standing up to huge footballers, getting tossed around like I was one of their footballs. I was no more capable of defending myself than a deer would be from a lion. I was committed to keeping Songbird safe, so I fought with all I had in me to preserve her reputation.

Strangely enough, after the first year, these guys started calling me Chipper, and they stopped stuffing me into trashcans. I became their mascot. Most importantly, they left Songbird alone.

She wasn't happy about that. She loved the attention, but I got her through high school unscathed. I left for university, and my sister went on to become a pop star.

I only saw Songbird a few times over the next five years. She had risen to fame, and I had married and had a son. It wasn't until I read that Songbird had been jailed for smuggling drugs into Canada from Mexico after one of her concerts that I saw her again. She was bitter and unrepentant and told me to take my worthless ass elsewhere. I left her sitting there in the visitors' reception room, preening in her hand mirror.

Six years later I heard of her again. She had been in drug rehab and cleaned herself up. I decided to find her, hoping that I might be able to rescue our relationship.

What I found was Songbird, living in a posh condo, pregnant with her fifth surrogate baby. She had hit the big time once again, making millions from wealthy men married to sterile women yearning for a baby of their own.

Once again, my sister, Songbird, was laying her eggs in other people's nests.

*Tramp *Squirrel *Ballistic *Toque

OLD WRINKLE PUSS

Thoughts ricocheted off the walls of her mind like bullets in a ballistics chamber with nowhere to go. They were locked in, but she knew what she knew, and this was enough for her.

She had the fantastic dream again that night. The audience clapping as she answered correctly the next-to-final question. Then the last, which would net her a million dollars. The audience holding its breath; intense silence as the last question is asked. Her elation overwhelming because she already knew the answer before the question was even asked. Tears of joy cascading down her face.

Opening her eyes, she looked up to see the tarp had leaked again and the rain – not tears – was dripping like a broken faucet onto her face.

A voice … "Hey, Old Wrinkle Puss, time to get up. It's almost nine o'clock. Pack up and move along now. No day camping in the park. You know the rules," the friendly policeman called out.

She creaked like a rusty gate in the wind as she rose to her feet. Rolling up the tarp, stuffing it into the Thrifty's cart she had managed to snag, and pulling on her woollen toque, she managed to limp toward the park exit. She said, "Good morning, Frisky!" to the squirrel she believed to be her pet, as it ran across her path.

On her way to the church she hoped pancakes were on the menu. *If I get lucky again today, someone will give me a fiver. Then I can buy that lottery ticket – but not from Thrifty's!* she reminded herself.

And … because she knew what she knew, she remembered a time, years ago, when they called her a tramp.

Now they called her homeless. And because she knew what she knew, she smiled and thought … *Progress.*

*Umbrella *Yareta *Potato
*Forever *Yesterday

CASUALTY

Yesterday it rained hard. This morning it was a deluge. I hobbled the short distance from my apartment to the restaurant on the corner. I saw my old neighbour struggling to fold his umbrella down at the entrance to the café. He reminds me of an ancient yareta, tough and resilient.

"Here Joe. Let me help you with that," I said.

"Thanks, young fella," he muttered and handed the dripping mess to me. He walked through the door and left me standing in the rain.

It seemed to take me forever to fold that bloody thing down, as it was actually a huge beach umbrella. People pushed past me, and yeah, I heard them laughing. I didn't care. I was used to it. I always seem to be a laughing-stock now, what with my wrecked legs and penchant for the bizarre. I guessed today would be no exception. And as it turned out, it wasn't.

Joe called me over to his table. He was already eating his breakfast of steak and eggs. It freaked me out a little, as I am now a strict vegan after what I saw over there; starving people killing over a hunk of rotting meat, some even eating rats. Now, watching people snarf down dead animals really gets to me.

As I sat down, the waitress came over and said in a loud teasing voice, "Here he is again, ladies and gentlemen, the Vegan Vigilante. Fried potatoes and beans again for breakfast, Brandon?"

There were loud guffaws from the patrons. But something in me snapped. I stood up and took a defensive stance. Didn't I have the right to defend myself?

"You ignorant, dimwitted rabble," I hollered. "You can all laugh but George Bernard Shaw told it like it is."

Then with a voice I never knew I had, I quoted the great man: "While we ourselves are the living graves of murdered beasts, how can we ever expect ideal conditions on earth?"

There was a stunned silence that I took to be a flattering interlude, but no, out came the manager. "You are causing a disturbance again today, Brandon. Now off you go. Out now! Out!"

His mistake was grabbing me by the arm.

"No, no, don't do that!" I vaguely remember hearing Joe say. It was too late. I had the manager by the throat when the police pried me off him.

My doctor later told me. "You have got to get a hold of yourself, Brandon," he said. "You're lucky all charges were dropped this time. Are you still going to your meetings at the VA? PTSD is nothing to fool with, my friend."

I don't go to the restaurant anymore. I'm banned. I eat my morning breakfast of fried potatoes and beans at home now. Alone ...

*Generation *Coffee *Work
*Season *Nectar

IF SEASONS WERE GENERATIONS

It was sticky and hot, the end of the apple season. A sweet, rancid smell filled the air, and wasps buzzed around drunkenly having nipped at the rotting apple nectar. Most of the pickers had already departed back to the company shed, leaving only two men to finish loading the remaining boxes.

Tom held a huge apple in front of his face. "If I never see another apple in my life, it will be too soon." He flung the shiny, red orb away into the dirt, where it bounced a few times and then settled into its bed of dust like a forgotten thought, gone forever. "Goodbye apple season!" he shouted and then looked over to where his companion worker, Rip, stood silently watching.

Rip bent down and hauled the last box of apples to the company truck. "Seasons are like generations; they begin and end with lots in between," he said quietly. "We got to learn from them and enjoy them."

"What are you rattling on about man? We still got work to do. This is our final load." Tom slammed down the trunk lid of his old Chevy and got in behind the wheel. He shouted at Rip before he sped off, "See you at the loading dock."

After the boxes were off-loaded, the two sweat-covered men sat at the edge of the wooden dock wiping their faces with grey, grungy scarves that they pulled off their heads. They swung their legs over the edge of the platform, creating a slight breeze that only the pesky fruit flies could enjoy.

The bent office accountant with white hair as wispy as fog approached the two men. He held two manila envelopes in his arthritic hands. After a slight clearing of his throat he said, "Ah, here are your final earnings, Rip and Tom. The manager thanks you for sticking it out through the season, but due to unforeseen expenses, your bonuses will not be quite what you were promised."

"Naturally," Tom mumbled.

"Good luck. Hope to see you next year." The old man hobbled quickly away trying to outrun his apology to the two men.

"Let's get outta here," they said in unison.

Tom walked to his car and then stopped and looked over at Rip who had started walking slowly away. "Hey Rip, how 'bout going for a beer? Let's spend some of that hard-earned money, eh?"

"Sounds good to me. I'm a coffee man myself," Rip replied.

"Hop in then."

As they drove down dirt roads to the highway, both men seemed to settle into themselves. Deep sighs escaped like air leaking from a worn, used tire. Not a word was said as they untwined into a short season of stillness.

*Miasma *Obnoxious *Soliloquy
*Forgetful *Teapot

THE HOMILY

She was round like a giant teapot and her spout drizzled out her obnoxious venom, raging against the three big M's, as she termed them: Miracles … Machines … and Men.

She no longer trusted any of them.

This was her miasmatic mantra, her soliloquy shouted aloud as she sat alone in her padded cell with only an audience of silence and unforgiving, forgetful, indifferent time.

Once she had been beautiful.

*Allegory *Vibration *Phalange*
Independence *Nesting

THE INTERLOPERS

"Why are we working on Independence Day?" The younger of the two construction workers asked.

The grey-bearded man just shook his head. "You work when necessary, no matter what day it is, dummy. Have you never heard the allegory of the ox in the mire?"

"Huh?" came from the brawny kid.

"Go figure," mumbled the older man.

It is a shame though, he thought, *disturbing the nesting grounds of the starlings with the vibration of the excavating machinery. They call this progress.*

Our boarded-up perimeter reminds me of the phalanges of old when armies of knights would cross their spears to create an impenetrable shield against the enemy invaders.

Only difference now, I guess, is that we are the invaders.

*Shower *Wedding *Sweater
*Forgiveness *Moon

THE DECISION

Her life had become as dark and lustreless as the night outside, her days as dreary.

As she examined her eye socket, which had already turned a sickly blue, she felt a strange burning sensation beginning to rise from her feet. Up, up it seared until even her head seemed on fire. She grabbed her head as if to put out the blaze. When she removed her hands, a clump of hair came too. As it fell into the sink, she knew that he would never again pull her by the hair out of the shower, out of the bed, or anywhere else.

She pulled a bathrobe around her wet, shaking shoulders and put Polysporin on her cracked lip and a band aid over the split above her right eye. She could do nothing to hide the bruises on her cheeks. But that did not matter anymore.

When she had decided something in the past, she always went through with it, but now as she looked into the mirror over the washbasin, she realized that the last decision she had made was her choice of wedding gown. That was five years ago.

She moved in a slow, deliberate way into the bedroom where she dressed in jeans and a heavy sweater. She knew he would not be back for hours.

He would be walking to town, to the bar, to meet his cronies and to commiserate, to grovel in self-pity. This he did to clear his mind, he always said. But she knew better. He did this to try to assuage his guilt. He always came back remorseful and pleading for her forgiveness. And she always acquiesced.

Not this time.

She did not pack anything into her bag that was not hers five years ago. Her handbag held only her cosmetics, cell phone, and driver's licence. She had no credit or bankcards. He handled all the money. But the gas tank was full, and she knew she would drive until it was empty.

There was only one way to go. The gravel road led through the town to the highway.

He had left over an hour ago, so she knew she would not pass him on the road. He would already be in the dim, smoke-filled bar.

Breathing a deep sigh of relief, she started off. As the headlights cut through the darkness, she began to feel an exhilaration mounting, almost as if she would explode. "I'm free!" she shouted wildly. "I'm free!"

At this instant she saw him walking right down the middle of the road, straight towards the car. He must have changed his mind and was coming back. She braked.

Did I really brake? The thought passed silkily through her mind like the dark cloud passed over the hidden moon, which now shone down in innocent splendour.

She opened her purse, pulled out her cell phone, and dialled 911. "I would like to report an accident."

Essential *Sunflower* *Clandestine*
Florist *Airport*

MISTAKEN IDENTITY

He had a face like a clock in pursuit of time – flat, relentless, and indifferent. His exactness and attention to detail made him a much sought-after political assassin. Governments used him in clandestine, hush-hush operations all around the world. He lived everywhere. No one knew his identity.

So, imagine his surprise when one morning between assignments, as he sat sipping coffee at Starbucks, a woman plunked herself down across from him.

She whispered, "You're early. I thought I was supposed to meet you at ten. Never mind. Here's a note with the location and the money. Ten thousand right?"

She shoved an envelope toward him. "My husband won't know what hit him. Good riddance to the bastard! Remember, it's essential that you do it today. Best ten thousand I ever spent! The conditions are all arranged." She jumped up and was gone before he could collect his thoughts.

"What the hell?" was all he said before he slipped the envelope into his vest-pocket, stood up, and made his way to the door. As he left the café, he noticed a young man sitting at a corner table, looking at his watch, annoyance written on his face.

"Hah! I get it. That punk's waiting for her. Sorry bud. Mistaken identity."

Just to be sure, he strolled a few doors down and entered a florist shop. He studied the displays of flowers and bags of peat moss, while eying the door.

"Can I help you?" the shopkeeper asked.

"Oh, yes, I'll take a dozen of the sunflowers."

"You going to a party, sir?"

"Yes, a party."

"Here you are, sir. That will be sixteen dollars."

He handed over a twenty. Before the shopkeeper could make change, he was gone out the back door into the alleyway. He took the note from the envelope and tore it up and then threw it and the sunflowers into a garbage bin. He made his way onto a busy street a few blocks further down.

He hailed a cab.

"Legion on forty fifth."

"Yes, sir," from the cabbie.

He entered the games room, walked over to the donation box, and stuffed the money-laden envelope inside. Without looking at anyone, he walked back out to the waiting cab.

"Airport."

"You got it, mister," the driver replied.

He sat in first class with a glass of brandy in his hand and a pretty woman smiling at him. He leaned back, gave a great sigh, and knew his destiny held no vainglory or delusion. His life was what it was.

*Mist *Persuasion *Amber
*Elysium *Vibrations

THE LITTLE VOICE

The mist settled on the trees that morning like a shroud – cloying, grey, and threatening. It was as if some baleful, vindictive entity had slithered into the pale first light from some dark nether region.

If Victor had noticed the creeping murk, or if he had ever paid attention to premonition, that kind of gut feeling one gets from some warning place deep within, his day might have gone better; his life might not have changed forever. But … he didn't, and it did.

Victor was late for work as usual. His wife cautioned him about the road conditions, even used persuasion by promising him his favourite dinner, if only he would listen to the news warning of slippery road conditions and low visibility.

Victor would have none of it. "I have no time. I'm late already. God, woman, get off my back. See you tonight." He slammed out the door without a thought for her feelings, thinking only about how troublesome she was.

The light was amber, but Victor didn't slow down; instead he accelerated trying to beat the red light. His car hydroplaned on the rain-soaked intersection, twirling like a dervish. The oil truck broadsided him; a flash, an explosion, a white light, and Victor was on his way to his Elysium.

The inquiry board did a thorough vivisection of the dramatic accident and deemed it gross negligence on the part of Victor, who had caused the fatal crash. The oil truck driver's wife was awarded compensation by the courts, commensurate to her loss, at least monetarily.

Victor's wife now cooks his favourite dinner for the new man in her life, who listens to and feels the vibrations of that little voice within that says, "Be careful, pay me some heed."

*Lasso *Drooling *Justice
*Witness *Armchair

THE LASSO LOUNGE

The justice pounded his gavel again and again. He shouted, "I will have order in this courtroom!"

Slowly, the tumult settled as onlookers reluctantly took their seats and mumbled under their breaths, "No way this is a fair trial. He doesn't deserve the death penalty."

Other dissenters hissed, "He deserves to be sent to the Lasso Lounge."

As the next witness for the prosecution took the stand, there was silence. But at his first words of testimony, the rumble of protesting voices started up again, and this time the judge reached the satiation point.

He ordered the courtroom cleared, hollering, "Out! Out! All of you!"

In an aside to the lawyers, he said, "This has turned into a rabble. It will be a closed hearing from here on in. Some of these people are drooling for the noose. We will resume tomorrow."

He quickly left the bench and slammed into his chambers, not looking left nor right. He flopped into his well-worn armchair and gave a deep sigh.

He felt the cold nose of his devoted golden retriever on his clutched fists.

He relaxed and opened his hands to stroke his faithful pet, saying, "Oh, Sir Cavendish, the dimensions of this case defy reality. I can't imagine what public dissent a non-guilty verdict would create, can you? On the other hand, what chaos would a guilty verdict incite?"

The judge sat far into the night pondering his decision, with Sir Cavendish not stirring at his feet.

It was early morning when the telephone startled the sleeping judge and dog still in chambers. Both sat upright looking around in bewilderment. The judge got to his feet, stumbled over to his desk, and picked up the phone.

"Who found him? In his cell you say? Yes, yes, I understand." He hung up the phone.

"Poor bugger," he said quietly.

"No need now, Sir Cavendish, for my verdict of dismissal," he said, bending down to see a reflection of his glistening tears in the dog's eyes.

*Anguish *Ashtray *Pinwheel
*Vociferate *Voucher *Forgiveness

A VOUCHER'S EXPIRATION

Nettie Filgate knew that nothing would change his mind. She had tried vociferating tactics, such as arguing and yelling back at him, and the "poor me", forlorn, lugubrious look, while sitting in close proximity, hoping he would reach out to touch and comfort her. It was all to no avail.

He would not budge. He was too wrapped up in his own anguish; there was no room for hers. He was unable to portion out even a modicum of understanding and forgiveness.

His luggage sat by the door. His heavy-hearted sigh was all she heard from him as he picked up his bags and started out.

Nettie called out, "Rick, please don't go like this! Is there no forgiveness in your heart? I am suffering too!"

Rick turned. The look he gave Nettie said it all. It was filled not only with anger, but also a deep loathing that turned his hazel eyes black.

Nettie cried out in alarm. "Is there no going back, Rick? It was an accident. I was exonerated. She was my daughter too."

At this, Rick came at Nettie, fists raised. He caught himself in time, but Nettie would have preferred a beating rather than the accusing vitriol that sputtered like drops of flaming lava from his tight lips.

"You killed her as surely as if you had held a gun to her head. Yes, the courts found you not guilty of vehicular homicide, but I know that you were not paying attention when you ran over her in the driveway. You can never convince me otherwise. You are also dead to me, Nettie. I never want to see or hear from you again. I leave it all to you."

Rick slammed out into the dark night. He loaded his bags into the waiting taxi and did not look back at his home and wife of twenty years.

Nettie stood rooted to the spot for long minutes, and then she turned and walked into the study and sat at the desk, with her head bent into her folded arms. A wave of exhaustion swept over her.

She heard herself whisper, "He leaves it all to me. Ashes, only ashes."

Going to the filing cabinet, Nettie pulled out the marriage certificate, rolled it up like a scroll, and sobbed. "It was only a voucher, all these years, an exchange for goods and services rendered. Worthless now. Me too, worthless."

Hours later, Nettie crashed the empty brandy bottle to the floor. She tried to light a cigarette, but as she raised the lighter, her eyes fell on the rolled-up scroll.

She muttered, "What the hell …"

The flames lit the night sky and the wind twirled them like pinwheels. Firefighters tried to quell the angry inferno, but it was too late.

A pale grey, funereal dawn looked upon what was left. The building had collapsed; nothing remained of home and life, but a powdery residue that had settled into the basement's cement ashtray.

*Peninsula *Ridiculous *Liberty
*Ligature *Nefarious

GIORGIO

Like a peninsula that is almost surrounded by water and not quite an island, Giorgio was not quite the nefarious Mafioso he wanted to be. In fact, he could not even tie the ligature correctly on the captive rival gang member.

He had incurred the wrath of the Mafioso captains. They thought him ridiculous, and worse than that – stupid.

Because of Giorgio's ineptness, the Mafia Godfather had to appease the townspeople. He lifted the curfew, gave liberty to the captive gang member, and even signed a compromise with the rival boss.

What about Giorgio?

Well, only the fishes know for sure.

*Trait *Poignant *Cymbal *Pie
*Helicopter *Pigment

EXIT

The loose ceiling fan is rotating loudly and erratically, sounding like a helicopter in trouble, in danger of crashing. I imagine that I am on that helicopter; in point of fact, I wish I were on it; then it would all be over.

A cymbal is reverberating in my head. Its metallic clang echoing the last bitter words that passed between us before he left. This time is for good.

The darts of recrimination have pierced our hearts. How can two people survive constant blame for the death of a child?

The dissolution of a marriage, like an acid slowly eating away at trust and respect, is beyond tragic. It is utterly the antithesis of convivial. It is cataclysmic. But the death of a child is an abyss, a void.

The memories come crowding in at odd times; soft poignant memories, suffused with the colourful pigment of our child's youthful days. His beloved traits of character that were so endearing and the remembrance of the little things he loved – lemon pie, his little tow truck and his favourite storybook – break my heart.

My husband too, I am sure, has felt these things, but communication is impossible when the mountain of guilt and condemnation cannot be scaled.

It is better this way. Let him go too. I will survive. I will drink my grief and eat regret for the rest of my life. That is what mothers do.

*Intangible *Provoke *Jewel
*Imposter *Adoration

BEWARE OF SUGAR

He was said to be a jewel of a man by those for whom good looks made the man. These were they who felt privileged to meet him.

However, the mysterious, intangible quality of him provoked much speculation among those who felt he was too good to be true.

Who was he really? Where did he come from? These were the questions asked by the more sceptical. Some even thought he had a Machiavellian air about him, a sinister aspect that dripped sugared words from his lips as he spoke.

His dark eyes promised benevolence; his smile pledged allegiance; his total demeanour was one of understated elegance. No wonder he had many followers clinging to his every gesture, grin, and word. He professed generosity of heart. His very presence seemed a reflection of his sparkling spirit.

Until one day all the adoration was eclipsed by something he said. And … if he meant it, then he was an imposter, a monster of the most horrific kind.

Could this be a surreptitious approach to anarchy some astute listeners asked.

He had given a speech at the Community For Artistic Development Association. He advocated, in the strongest terms, that poetic and artistic licence must be done away with. In its place, only facts and factual, proven theories should be allowed. Vocabulary should be strictly limited to only government-approved words.

Had he morphed into an Orwellian? Or had he been one all along?

A great shout of "Imposter," echoed throughout the crowd of artists.

Suddenly doors were thrown open, and armed men in black uniforms stormed in. They surrounded the group of terrified spectators. And the jewel of a man said, "Ladies and gentlemen, meet the NEW WORLD ORDER."

*Falsify *Justify *Apple pie
*Timbre *Hut

A PERFECT TEMPLATE

They have just finished the main course of their lunch at the White Spot Restaurant.

"I'm filled with indecision," Penny says. "Shall I have apple pie à la mode or with whipped cream, or maybe the lemon tart for dessert?"

"What's the difference? It all goes to the same place." Then in a low aside he says, "Straight to your derriere."

"I heard that, Angus." She looks around to see if anyone else has heard his rude remark.

There are smirks on the faces of some men at the next table but also some looks of distaste from women sitting nearby for what has been said.

"You know, Angus, I wonder how you justify it to yourself, make it all right, to speak to me like this."

He retorts, never to be outdone. "Did you not falsify your weight this morning when you filled out your driver's licence application? How do you justify that? You no more weigh 160 pounds than a 400-pound gorilla."

"Now you compare me to a gorilla?" Penny's ire is up and so is the timbre of her voice. She takes a deep breath – and another – and another – to calm herself.

The apple pie piled high with whipped cream is set before Penny. "Thank you," she says to the waiter. Then she looks over at Angus and goes on.

"I suppose to justify and to falsify are both a certain form of dishonesty."

"How do you figure that?" He is sputtering in indignation. "I am not at all dishonest."

"My lying about my weight doesn't hurt anyone but me. It shows my insecurity, thinking I do not fit the perfect mould. Whereas your hurtful remarks show a distain for me, your wife, who has born you five children. You have lied to yourself, thinking that you have the inalienable right to be verbally abusive and sarcastic. You believe you are somehow exempt from good manners and above the rest of humanity. You have a tiny hut of a mind filled with nothing but hot air."

She goes on gaining momentum then stops to adjust her verbal outrage to one of action.

"You have also lied to these people at the next table, saying that this apple pie will end up on my ass."

She stands, takes the dish of apple pie, piled high with whipped cream, and smashes it onto the top of Angus's head. "There, justify that!"

As she leaves the restaurant, there is whispered "Bravos" from the adjoining table where sit three ladies who also fit the perfect template of true womanhood.

*Aromatic *Calendar *Cumbersome
*Uncanny *Wood tick

A DOODLE

My appointment book is not a slick, neatly bound ledger but rather a sixty-page ratty scribbler in which I try to keep a few pages for a calendar of sorts. It is cumbersome but somehow comforting as it's been with me for ages. It acts as a journal and idea resource because I write down little snippets of quotes and observations, not to mention doodles. I love to doodle. I doodle when I am on the phone or watching the news.

I used to doodle boxes, but now it seems I doodle whatever I hear. For example, the other night I listened to a newscast about a child who became very ill and was about to die, when the mother found a wood tick in her hair that doctors and hospital personnel had missed. The child recovered, but strangely I doodled wood ticks for weeks afterwards.

Yesterday, I went to a spa, and as I lay waiting for the massage therapist, I thought of an old flame who I had almost married. He was handsome and that is about all I can remember of his characteristics.

Now lying prone, naked with a soft cover over me and the aromatic scent of exotic oils soothing my senses, I am almost in nirvana. I hear the door open, and I am greeted by a silky voice saying, "Good afternoon. I hope you are comfortable."

I jerk out of my reverie, and lo and behold, there he is, still handsome but now maybe he has developed more and better attributes and skills. Uncanny meeting him again in this position, but hey, it is what it is.

I wonder what I will doodle tonight?

*Clusters *Clock *Preposterous
*Fungus *Soiree *Soliloquy

TICK TOCK

There is a word for the inciting incident; a word that evokes feelings of impossible odds, a word that is so contrary to reason as we define it, so utterly devoid of common sense as to make the intellect stagger. The word is "PREPOSTEROUS".

Everyone who later read about the occurrence said it was preposterous!

But ... those who were there used no such word to describe what they had witnessed.

The crowd had broken into clusters, some bearing placards that read "Hang the traitor," others shouting, "Death to the murderer," while still others singing hymns accompanied by a brass band.

The silent onlookers paid no heed to the crowd, but looked anxiously at the grand, ornate clock upon the brick wall of the prison. The clock was illuminated by bright rainbow-coloured lights, which seemed to mock the sombre reality of the impending execution.

At 11:56 p.m., the floodlights surrounding the crowd brightened. A hush came over the spectators. Even the air seemed to hold its breath. A steel gate creaked open, and the youthful prisoner appeared between two prison guards.

The young man walked of his own accord, head held high, a face as placid and shining as the new moon. He mounted the steps to the gallows quickly, as if going to a much-anticipated soiree. The crowd gasped at such a show of nonchalance.

Upon reaching the platform, the young man paused and seemed to enter a private space. He spoke in quiet soliloquy, his lips moving as if in prayer. Then he surveyed the crowd.

He shouted, "Once again I say I am innocent of the crime for which I will be hung. God have mercy on your souls!"

Some in the crowd jeered, others hung their heads in deference to his words, while others wept silently, nodding assent.

The hangman, who with an evil smile draped the noose around the young man's neck, said quietly, "You'll soon be part of the fungus that rots organic matter. Guilty or not, you little freak, I'll break your neck!" He pulled the trap door open.

A slight crack and it was over.

The crowd drew in its breath and let it out in a rush. Noisy prattle and anguished sobs echoed in the night air. Suddenly all the lights went out except for the colourful lights around the huge clock. The clock had stopped at midnight. There began a great rumbling as if a freight train were running through the throng.

Then a penetrating stillness ...

A soft white cloud descended from above, encompassing the still form of the hanging young man, obliterating him from the sight of the onlookers.

The floodlights came back on. The indrawn breath of the spectators sucked the oxygen out of the surrounding space at what they saw! The noose, swaying at the end of the sturdy rope was now... empty!

Suddenly the massive clock started ticking loudly, "tick tock" ... "tick tock" ... until people had to cover their ears. Still they heard it, louder and louder!

They scattered and ran pell-mell, brass instruments flung aside, placards trampled underfoot until all that was left of the crowd were the silent ones, who had knelt to pray in thanksgiving for the redemption of their innocent boy.

"PREPOSTEROUS!" Screamed the newspapers as the story leaked out.

But... those who had witnessed the phenomenon were and still are in mute awe. If they speak of it at all, they say the word "MIRACLE"!

*Sea *Bender *Storm
*Angry *Still

A FICKLE MASTER

Erik loved the sea.

Pop had taken the fishing vessel out early yesterday morning. Erik had been on a bender the night before, so when Pop tried to rouse him in the early hours, he snarled, "Leave me be, dammit!" And so, Pop had sailed off by himself.

The storm had hit mid-afternoon, and Erik knew it was a bad one.

No sign of Pop.

Early evening came – no sign of Pop.

Black, angry night – no sign of Pop.

Now, two weeks later – still no sign of Pop.

Erik looked down from the rocky cliff – high tide rushing in.

The white-capped foaming waves crashing against the steep cliffs seemed to be hammering in his brain, "He's gone. He's gone." The words echoed in his tortured mind.

One step and he was free-falling.

His only thought, "I'm sorry, Pop."

PART THREE
{MRS. LEWIS' SHORT STORIES}

*Sister *Art *Charm *Dog
God Catastrophe

DANCER

My sister doesn't like me. Never has. Even as kids she would berate me and call me names. My parents would say, "Don't bother your baby brother, Rose dear. He is so little." Because she is older I have had to develop a way to get back at her, hold my own, so to speak. Over the years I have perfected my strategy to a fine art. I take great pleasure in annoying her and watching her reactions to my ingenious schemes. She is no innocent either, I might add. She has her uppity ways of sticking it to me too.

I blame my mother and father for this antipathy between us. My parents called her the "Uptown Girl". As a result, she came to believe she was just a little better than almost anyone else, me included of course. Did I mention her name is Rose? "Darling Rose," my mother would say, "you can go far with your looks and charm, but always remember who you are."

Well, she has remembered and then some. She lives in a posh condo right in the centre of the city. She is a fashion designer with her own brand name. She also has a young, female French poodle named Josette. She takes the dog to the doggie salon every few weeks and, of course, boasts about the white, fluffy fur coat it has. I don't blame the dog for being a little aloof. She is only emulating Rose.

I've got a dog too, by the way. His name is Dancer. He is a Chinese crested hairless breed, naked as a jaybird, with bare, pale skin mottled like a leopard or an old man covered with liver spots. He does have some hair though; shaggy grey hair sprouts like weeds gone wild on his head, ears, and feet. I rescued him from the breeder who was going to "bucket" him. I was in the right place at the right time that day. I always thank God for that. Just as the breeder was about to drown the poor little newborn in a bucket of water, I yelled, "Stop! What the hell are you doing?" The breeder growled, "Look at the little bastard. He's butt ugly and a runt to boot."

"I'll take him, dammit, and pay full price too, you jerk. You have no heart, man."

So this is how I became the owner of the most plug-ugly little creature on the planet. He is also the best friend I ever had. Why, he is so friendly that I swear he is human. This is why I have trained him to dance and laugh out loud, showing his buckteeth in a huge grin. He is the joy of the old folks home where we visit every week, and the kids at the hospital come alive when he dances and laughs for them. Yeah, this twelve-inch-high, ten-pound, spirited, little guy even gives hugs with his paws entwined around the kids' necks.

My sister tells me that we make a good pair. "Well matched and extremely apt," she snickers behind her elegant manicured hand. "Make sure you don't bring him into my home. He may hurt my Josette." Again she laughs. "Yes, a perfect pair."

"You're right, Rose, of course," I reply and vow to somehow get even for her biting remark. How I do it is unbelievable and totally unplanned.

Two days later: Catastrophe!

"Hey, Doc, something's really wrong with my dog," I am yelling over the phone.

"Bring him in right away, Doug, and we'll find out what's wrong," he replies.

I bundle Dancer up in a blanket and rush over to the vet's office.

The vet takes us into his room right away, and I lay Dancer on the table.

"What seems to be the trouble?" he asks sympathetically.

"Well, Doc, yesterday at the park he went after another male dog."

"That's not unusual, Doug. Male dogs do fight. Was he bitten somewhere?"

"Ugh, no, Doc, he, well, he didn't exactly fight. He, ugh, got fresh with the other dog." I am stammering like a jackhammer trying to explain the situation.

The vet smiles and nods. "Well, Doug, many animals display what we refer to in layman's language as "same-sex tendencies". It happens in dogs too. You might say Dancer is of the pink persuasion." He laughs and winks at me. "Has he been neutered?"

"Hell no, I would never put him through that."

"Well, Doug, it seems you won't have to worry on that account now, will you?" Again he laughs and pats me on the back. He picks Dancer up and Dancer gives him one of his toothy laughs and famous hugs.

Sheepishly, I leave the office and proceed home with my little gay friend.

The next night I get a frantic call from Rose. She has been called out of town to a business conference. "I can't find anyone on such short notice to mind Josette. Can you possibly stay over with her for two days?" She is using her svelte, persuasive voice that catches me in its silky web once again.

"Okay, I'll be right over." I bundle up Dancer in his soft, woollen jacket and head out.

The two days go by really fast, and it isn't the big deal I thought it would be. Josette and Dancer get along all right, and when we walk outdoors, they are both very circumspect and polite. Maybe Dancer is learning something from Josette for he seems more subdued than usual. A real gentleman I think.

Yeah, a real gentleman, I think, until one night a month later when Rose is pounding on my door screaming bloody murder. I open the door and there she is, holding Josette, who seems a lot fatter, in her outstretched arms. "You have ruined her. Your ugly mutt got her pregnant. Now she is your responsibility." Rose pushes Josette into my arms and abruptly leaves, muttering, "Ludicrous losers, all three of you."

I'm in big trouble. Now I've got two dogs, Dancer and Josette. And, how many more when Josette gives birth? I only have to wait four weeks and I find out. Twelve! And boy, are they ugly little beggars.

Strangely enough though, it isn't so bad. Josette is a good mother and Dancer an even better one. He licks and nuzzles each pup. He picks them up by the scruff of their necks and shoves them back into the huge basket when they tumble out. Then he climbs in with them and cuddles them about him, almost purring in contentment.

At ten weeks, the pups are very rambunctious, and I know I somehow have to get rid of them, find them good homes. But how? Who would want them? They look like goblins.

As this thought hits me, another explodes in my mind. It is almost Halloween. I'll advertise goblins for sale to good homes.

It is working like a charm. My phone hasn't stopped ringing. Kids are begging their parents for one of the pups/goblins.

"A real live goblin! Daddy, please buy it for me," I hear over and over.

Of course I make every sale with a return policy, and all must sign a home inspection document before I allow any of the goblins out of my sight.

Eleven gone. One to go. This female pup is smaller and more crinkled than the rest, even uglier than Dancer, who has taken a great interest in the pup's well-being and never leaves its side.

One morning, I wake up to find that pup on my pillow, deposited there by Dancer I am sure. It is looking at me with the most beseeching stare, soft green eyes boring into mine. My heart turns over, and I know she is begging me to keep her. I laugh real loud and cuddle that puppy. I swear Dancer knew I would decide to keep her. The pup also knows I'm keeping her, for in her excitement she is peeing all over me.

Now, what to name her? The old retaliation devil is working overtime in my brain. Finally I give in to the temptation. I will call her Rose. I can hardly wait to introduce her to my sister.

Oh, yeah. One final note to myself, kind of a double indemnity:

- Get two spayed. Sorry girls!
- One neutered – just in case Dancer decides to go over to the other side for good

*Innate *Shark *Propensity
*Blithering *Idiot *Naïve

REVENGE OF THE COWS

Merribelle Watkins had an innate ability to see through people. She concentrated on the heart. If there were tiny cracks on the surface, she would know that this person knew what life was all about. It indicated that they had suffered loss and had moments of joy – for both split the heart with tiny fissures. You see the heart cannot hold the immensity of both. If, however, the heart was tight and smooth, she knew that the person was hard-hearted and arrogant.

She could see no cracks on Willie Jack's heart, and when he shook her hand that first day, she almost screamed, for his hand too was hard and calloused and maybe even dangerous.

"You don't look like any veterinarian I ever saw," Willie said as he grasped her hand in a vise-like grip. "More like a Playboy Bunny, I'd say."

"Well, I am a vet, and what is it you have called me about?" Merribelle asked. She shook her head in disgust.

"It's my herd of dairy cows. They are acting strange these last few days. Come on to the barn, and I'll show you."

The barn was filthy. The cows were in stalls reeking with excrement and black mould. Merribelle entered the first stall. As she bent to examine the cow's udders she saw great bruises on them.

"What has happened here?" she asked.

"Oh, that's old Bossie. She gets out of hand sometimes and has to be taught a lesson."

"And so you hit her?"

"Just a friendly kick to remind her who's boss, that's all."

"Mr. Jacks, I may have to report this to the humane society."

"Aw, now why would a pretty little thing like you do something like that?" he said as he sidled up to Merribelle.

"I want these cows put out into the pasture right now, understood? I will examine all of them. Your license is in jeopardy, Mr. Jacks.

"Aw, come on, call me Willie, won't you?" Again he came close enough for her to smell the liquor on his fetid breath.

"Immediately, Mr. Jacks!" she ordered.

When the cows were released into the overgrown pasture Willie stormed into his shabby house, muttering under his breath.

Merribelle went among the herd and was appalled at their condition. She went back once more to Bossie. As she patted Bossie's head, she heard a whispering sound. Merribelle looked around to see who had spoken, but there was no one there. Again she heard it.

"It's me, Bossie. Merribelle I'm trying to talk to you."

Merribelle stood frozen, not believing what she had heard. "Is it possible that you are talking to me, Bossie, and I can understand you?"

"Yes, yes, at last salvation. Please help us. Willie is a monster. So cruel. He kicks us and beats us every day. He bought a milking machine that he tortures us with by tightening it so we bawl. He is a devil. We are trying to find a way to get away from him."

"I am not sure what I can do right away to relieve your pain, but I will go to work on a solution. Meanwhile try to bear up, Bossie."

"There are twenty-five of us all called stupid names starting with the letter B. What kind of a fool would call a cow Bossie or Bessie or Bonnie or Buttercup or Bluebird or … The list goes on and on. It is an insult to our intelligence. We cannot go on like this for much longer."

"I will try my utmost to help you, I promise," Merribelle said, but it may take some time."

"Time is what we do not have, but thank you for the offer. How is it that someone finally understands me?" Bossie asked.

"I do not know. I have other strange abilities, so I have gotten over my initial surprise. I have a propensity for the unusual. People's first impression of me is that I am a naïve, pretty doll, but underneath I am a fighter. I can roll over these kinds of men like a Sherman tank. We will work together to save your lovely herd of cows. I must go now, but I will be back." Merribelle patted Bossie's head.

That night, Willie herded the cows into the barn and whipped them. Afterwards, he stumbled out into the meadow in his drunken stupor. Bossie quieted the others and said, "We must fight him." She pulled at the latch that held the barn door tight. Finally it released, and she led the cows out one by one. They saw Willie in the meadow yelling at the moon like the blithering fool he was.

One by one the cows silently surrounded Willie. At a signal from Bossie, they closed in upon him, pushing him to and fro, and not gently. They raised their voices and shouted accusations at him, which he, even in his drunken state, understood. Willie's surprise burst from him in curses, but the cows continued to batter him, stepping on his toes, biting at his legs. Finally Bossie lifted her leg and kicked him hard in his udders. He went down hard.

The cows strolled out to pasture under the stars, breathing in the night, sighing in praise of the Creator, knowing that somehow things would change.

Willie, after limping out to his truck the following morning, yelled at the herd, still musing in the meadow, "I'll be back, and you'll see who is boss!"

The doctor examined Willie and said it would be some time before he would be healed, but after Willie ranted on about what the cows had called him, the doctor shook his head and thought Willie needed more help than a simple doctor could give. He recommended a psychiatrist friend of his. This put Willie in a rage, and he left the doctor's office ranting about what the cows had called him.

The doctor called his friend and said, "Have I got one for you!"

When Willie got back to the farm, he once again shut the cows in the barn and threatened to burn it down. But instead he once again beat on them, especially Bossie.

It was pitch dark when Bossie finally was able to unlatch the barn door. Again, one by one, the cows filed out. This time they made a semi-circle under the bedroom window where Willie snored like a buzz saw. Bossie started the serenade with a low hum. The others took up the note. Soon the night was alive with sound. Willie woke up and came to the window. Just then the moon peeked out from the night clouds. What Willie saw made his jaw drop. What he heard sent shivers through him.

The cows sang an old World War Two song: "We'll meet again. Don't know where, don't know when, but we know we'll meet again another day."

Merribelle came that morning with an order to have the dairy farm suspended and Willie charged with cruelty to animals. Willie had to sell the farm and herd at auction to pay court fees. Merribelle showed another hidden talent that day. Like a shark, she was able to outsmart and outbid other hopefuls and thus won the farm and herd.

Bossie petitioned Merribelle for new names for the herd. "Something delicate and distinguished please, like Catherine spelled with a 'C' for me and maybe Elizabeth and Louisa, and… she went on until all the cows had the names of their desires.

Meanwhile Willie is out on bail. He walks, still gingerly, down the streets, mumbling about the talking and singing cows and repeating the names they called him. People shake their heads and give him a wide berth. Rumour has it that Willie wears an athletic cup night and day to prevent another kick to his udders.

*Sweetheart *Delicate *Potential *Potato
*Box *Water *Diamonds

THE SWEETHEART CRUISE

Walking down the crowded avenue I am deep in thought wondering how I am going to "pop" the question.

I've never been a charismatic kind of dude, lavishing little gifts and trinkets on her. I'm kinda belligerent at times, I will admit. But, hey, you gotta be able to fight your battles and hold your own in this crummy world, wouldn't ya think?

Somebody gently bumps my arm as I start across the street. It's an old dude. "Oh, so sorry, son," he says, and then he trips.

I grab his arm. "I gottcha, Pops!" I help him the rest of the way across the busy street. The walk sign is orange, and cars start beeping their horns. Drivers give us the finger out their windows as we slowly make our way to the other side.

"Hey, old fella, shouldn't you be using a cane or something to get around?" I ask.

I let go of his arm, and he wobbles. I grab him again and guide him over to a bench on the side of the sidewalk.

I ask the same question and he says, "Well I had a good cane made of oak wood, my father's old cane that he carved himself, but yesterday some ruffians pushed me down, and darned if they didn't take that cane with them. Don't know what use it is to them, but there it is."

I pat the old man's arm. Something comes outta my mouth that gob-smacks me, "You can't do without a cane. How about we get in my car, and I drive you to Canadian Tire and we get you a new cane?"

"I'd like that, son, but I am low on funds just now."

Again I surprise myself. "No problem, Pops. It's on me."

"Much obliged," he says with a grin the width of his jaws and then some. So off we go.

Here I am again, the next day, walking down that same street and think-ing the same thought. How and where am I going to "pop" the question?

I hear a shout. "Sonny, over here." There is the same old man, grinning ear to ear, sitting on the same bench.

Strangely, I feel glad to see him. I go over and sit beside him. "How you doin', Pops?" I say.

"I'm fine, just fine, but you, my boy, seem to be troubled. What's the problem?"

I've never been one to yap about what bothers me, but for some reason I start blurting out the thing that's driving me nuts.

"Ya see … uh … I got this girlfriend and … uh … well, I want to marry her, but I just don't know how and where to pop the question."

"Son, that shouldn't be a problem. Just ask her! What's holding you back?"

"It needs to be somewhere special, like romantic you know."

"Mmm, I see. I asked my wife to marry me one day while we were pad-dling down the gorge waterway; right there I asked her. She was so excited that she jumped up, and didn't we end up swimming to shore? We made a big splash so to speak! Thereafter, we both called our adventure the "Sweetheart Cruise". It was a never-ending, funny memory for us, I tell you."

We are laughing so hard that the bench teeters. I wipe the tears from my eyes and pound the old man's back.

"That's the most crazy thing I've ever heard. How could I possibly top that one?" I say, giggling like a schoolgirl.

Then it hits me. *Why not try it?* The thought takes hold, and I start plan-ning. I say goodbye to the old man and feel light as a feather. This weekend … canoeing on the gorge. The Sweetheart Cruise! Perfect!

I shake the old man's hand, and as I walk off, I say aloud, "This will have the potential of being a hilarious, lifelong memory, just like the old man's."

It's Saturday morning. We are out on the water. I am paddling at a good speed. I know I have to be delicate in my approach, tough for me, but I will give it a good try. The small blue box is burning a hole in the pocket of my cut-off shorts. I look at Sadie sitting there, facing me, gazing at me, her hand trailing in the cool water. The sun is hot, and I'm starting to sweat. Sadie too has beads of sweat like small diamonds sitting on her forehead. *It's now or never,* I tell myself.

My hands are shaking as I lay the paddles down. I reach awkwardly into my pocket for the little box. I'm going to open it in front of her just like I have seen it done in the movies. I will watch her eyes open in surprise as she realizes what is about to happen. Then tears of love will cascade down her face as she smiles and gushes, "Yes."

"What's wrong, Daniel?" she asks as I am squirming, trying to get the box out of my pocket. "Did something bite you?"

"No," I say grouchily just as the box decides to come out. I fumble it in both of my hands like it's a hot potato then grab it hard. Sadie gasps knowing what it is. Before I can speak, she jumps toward me. The weight of her knocks my hand, and the box goes into the water.

The box floats a little way off, but Sadie is already swimming after it.

"What the hell!" I say and I jump in too. We paddle around awhile till I can grab the box. We face each other laughing, treading water.

As I open the box, and take out the ring, she screams, "Yes!"

Still treading water, I put the ring on her finger. No need to say, "Will you marry me?"

Back on dry land, the canoe floating away on the current with the little blue box not far behind, I think, 'That wasn't so bad, and she did say 'yes'."

For months now I've been walking down that same sidewalk, hoping to see the old man so I can tell him about our Sweetheart Cruise, but he's never there. The disappointment sits in me like a heavy iron anchor. I don't even know his name. I regret this more than anything in my life up to this point.

This regret eats at me. Why didn't I ask him his name?

Then yesterday as I walked by the bench where we sat I felt someone touch me on my shoulder. I looked around, but there was no one there.

Then he says to me like a voice out of the blue, "Call me 'Angel'." And so I do, to this very day, especially when my wife and I laughingly remember our own Sweetheart Cruise.

*Insanity *Pumpernickel *High jinks
*Family *Implode

FRIENDS

I'm being interrogated, but I can't see the man clearly. His voice is persuasive and soft like distant thunder. I'm not afraid, but I wonder what I'm doing here.

"You say your name is George?"

"Yeah."

"Full name if you please."

"Um ... George Lionel Giuseppe Abram Edwards."

"You seem to hesitate. Is this your real name? You must be completely honest here. Do you understand?"

"Yeah, I understand. I hesitated because it has been a long time since anyone asked me my full name, and I'm kinda shy about it, you know. Got lots of ribbing about it cuz it's so long. The whole family's represented so to speak."

"There's nothing wrong with family."

"Oh yeah, I know that."

"Well, we agree on that. Now let's move on. You were yelling for somebody called Andrew when you arrived. What's that all about?"

"I don't rightly know. It's kinda foggy."

"Let's start at the beginning. Who is this Andrew? Tell me about him."

"Andrew's my best friend. I don't want you to think that he is bonkers or insane like some folks have said. It's just that he is …"

"Go on."

"Just a minute, if you don't mind, sir. I'm searching for the right word … mmm … different. Yeah, different. His mind is kinda dark and dense like a loaf of pumpernickel. But don't get me wrong; he's loyal especially to friends and animals and that means a lot to me."

My interrogator is silent, so I go on. "We had been living in this six-storey, cement mammoth of a building for six years when, out of the blue, the manager sez that the building will be imploded in two months. So there we were, all of the residents scrambling for new digs. Well, Andrew and I just couldn't find a new place to live, too expensive. I kept looking, but Andrew, he just sat with his head in his hands crying and saying, 'What are we going to do, George, and what about Snickers? Who's gonna let us in with a dog?' That's how it was, no prospects and Andrew carrying on like that."

For some reason, there I am blubbering just remembering how sad Andrew was. My interrogator clears his throat almost like he's feeling it too.

"That's a sad situation, George. But do go on. What happened then?"

"Well, seems heaven smiled on us, for the very next day, a guy says he has a boathouse for rent. He called it a 'float home'; you know, it sounds a little more highfalutin, but I didn't care. I just rushed off to tell Andrew the good news, and even better, we could bring Snickers with us."

"How did Andrew react when you told him the good news?"

"He was some happy, I can tell you, jumping up and down and hugging me. Snickers was barking and drooling all over us. We loaded our stuff into a rental van and made our way to the waterfront. It was kinda disappointing when we saw where the boat was, in weeds and shallow river water, but we noticed there was a wooden pier going out to it. 'You think this is a high jinks, George?' Andrew asked me.

"I said, 'No it's no joke. It will be okay.' So, we unloaded our stuff and then returned the van and hailed a cab back to the river. This almost broke us, but we said we'd figure the finances out tomorrow. We went to our bunk beds early when the rain started. It was heavy, but we both love the sound of rain. Snickers settled down too.

"Now here's where it gets dicey because a fog seems to be coming over me and I can't remember clearly what happened next." I pause and look around me. There are other folks being questioned at other stations, and all are talking and explaining about why they are here. The voice of the interrogator seems even softer now.

"Go on, take your time remembering, George. This is very important. What happened next?"

I take a deep shuddering breath and go on. "It must have been about midnight when all of a sudden the boat starts rocking. Andrew yells, 'What the hell is happening, George?' I can't say cuz I don't know. We rush out onto the small wooden patio on the front of the boathouse and there we are floating down the river. Snickers is barking his head off. Andrew is shouting, and there we are reeling like a drunk down the avenue of river. The rain has stopped, and there is a slice of moon way up there. Suddenly, part of the patio gives way. Snickers and I slide off into the river. I reach up, but can't grasp onto what's left of the patio. Andrew is hanging there reaching out. Snickers bobs up beside me.

"I call out, 'Help me, Andy, I can't swim!' Andrew pauses for just a moment. He yanks Snickers by the scruff of the neck back onto what's left of the shattered patio. I go under for the second time."

My interrogator does not speak.

"Are you there?" I ask.

There is a long interval before once again the voice speaks. "You must be understanding where you are now, George."

"Yeah, I'm getting the picture, sir. What now?"

"It's up to you, George. You must hate Andrew for choosing to save Snickers instead of you."

"What do you mean? Hate Andrew? No way, no siree! We are friends. He just loved that dog a little bit more than me, that's all."

I look up and there he is, my interrogator, his smile brighter than any light I ever seen.

"Welcome home, my friend, George Lionel Giuseppe Abram Edwards!"

*Angel*Piffle*Character
*Sideways*Donkey*Anon

THE BRIDGE

Do you believe that some things in life are insurmountable? Or do you believe that there are the exceptional few who can turn mouse pellets into gold nuggets?

Well, let me tell you about someone who did just that.

The baby boy was born to Margaret Maynor and Eric Key on February 5, 1980. This was a momentous occasion for the parents, as they had waited five years for this day. Of course they were ecstatic to welcome the little angel into the world.

"His name will be the most important attribute of his life, so we must be careful to name him well. It will build his character," said Eric.

"Oh piffle!" Margaret said. "You can't tell me that a name means that much, for heaven's sake! Where did you learn such drivel? He will be called 'Donald'!"

"You may think I have a sideways view of this, but I assure you, my dear, that our son will have a name that will make him strong and invulnerable to life's challenges. He should have a great name. Yes, a great name – 'Joseph'," Eric said.

And so it went on back and forth for five days. Finally, Eric gave in and shouted, "Well, what will we call him? He's almost an old man for crying out loud! You name him then."

"Now, Eric, don't be melodramatic! I really think it should be 'Donald'. I love the name. I have loved it ever since I was a little girl and went to see a cartoon with Donald Duck. I have my heart set on it. Eric, please let's call our baby 'Donald'." Margaret looked at Eric with soft, tear-filled eyes.

So, what could the poor man do? He acquiesced and sighed. "'Donald' it is." Then holding the baby high in the air, Eric said, "There my son, I hope the name will make you strong."

The adamant stance of the father was inverted.

The baby boy was so sweet that soon he was nicknamed 'Donny'. Donny went to playschool, kindergarten, primary, and on into middle school with that appellation. He was popular and intelligent. He played soccer. He learned to sing and play piano, drums, and guitar. Donny was invited to birthday parties every week, it seemed. He was a fulfilled happy boy, and his parents were very proud of their Donny.

It was during the summer before high school that Donny decided that he wasn't a baby anymore and insisted he be called 'Don'. He felt it was more grown-up.

Eric supported his son and said to Margaret, "Let the boy choose, Margaret. He is a young man now. Let's not make issues where there are none." And so the family called him 'Don'.

It wasn't until high school began that the full implications of his insistence on being called 'Don' hit. It was during roll call on the first day of class that it started.

The teacher had called out the names of twenty-two students and then asked, "Did I miss anyone?"

Don put up his hand.

"Well, what is your name, young man?" the teacher asked.

"I'm Don."

"Don what? Full name, please. Don't waste my time. We must get on to other topics."

Don replied, "Don Key."

The teacher looked startled. Titters started and soon the room exploded with laughter. Even the teacher could not hide his grin. Someone brayed.

"Donald, Donald Key!" Red-faced, Don shouted, but his voice could not be heard above the hubbub. He had realized for the first time that his name was the butt of a joke.

What he couldn't have imagined were the implications this would have on his life. For from that moment of ridicule, he began to lose confidence in himself.

Little by little, for the next two years, Don shrivelled into himself, becoming shy and withdrawn. He took circuitous paths home after school so as not to be taunted with shouts of "Hey Donkey!" and loud braying or beatings by bullies. He became hyper-vigilant.

In the third year of high school, Don joined the football team. He was tall and strong so was accepted, but when the teasing followed him even there, he once again fell into himself. Most of his time was spent on the bench.

His parents had suspected that their son was troubled, but in all the three years, Don had never disclosed how he was being tormented at school.

It was after midnight when Eric was about to retire when he saw a light still on in Don's bedroom. He opened the door quietly, expecting to see that Don had fallen asleep while reading. What he saw drew a scream of anguish from him.

"Oh my God! My son! What have you done?"

Don lay in the fetal position on the floor, foaming at the mouth and convulsing, with five empty prescription bottles scattered about.

Margaret heard Eric and ran to him.

"Call 911. Margaret, hurry, hurry!"

A month later, when Eric entered the hospital room, Don was sitting in a chair, looking vacantly out of the window.

"Doc says you can come home today, son. You'll soon be able to go back to school and take up where you let off, my son."

"I'm not going back," Don said in a quiet voice.

"What's this then? Why not? What's going on, son? You haven't said why you tried to kill yourself. Let me help. We can get you help."

Suddenly Don was on his feet yelling, "No one can help, damn you! No one!" He smashed his fist on the window and glass and blood splayed around the room. He was shaking and sobbing.

Eric took the boy in his arms and stroked his hair saying, "Let it out Donny, let it out."

Eric and Margaret were furious when they finally understood what their son had endured. Margaret wanted to take Don out of school, but Eric said, "No, he would only have the same wherever he goes. He has to fight the bastards."

Father and son discussed the situation until it became clear what Don had to do. "You outsmart them, son, in every way. Only you will know how to do it. You are strong. Don't let them win!"

So Don went back to school and endured for yet a little while until he invented a strategy. He rejoined the football team. He said 'good morning' to his classmates and ignored their surprise at his familiarity.

It was when he wore the baseball cap and t-shirt emblazoned with the image of a donkey, which he had ordered specifically as part of his stratagem, that he got the upper hand. During roll call, he would say his full name loudly: Don Key. Attitudes began to change and humour took the place of derision.

One night, Eric announced that his brother, sister-in-law, and his niece were coming for a two-week visit. Don had not seen his cousin for over two years. The family had been living in France. When they arrived, Don was knocked off his feet at the sight of his cousin. She had grown into a stunning, young woman and her French accent was charming.

The following Friday, Don took her to the high school dance. Whereas before he had sat on the sidelines, this night he had all eyes riveted upon him and his cousin.

As they danced, he would be stopped by other couples asking, "Hey Donkey, who's your partner?"

Of course, Don did not say she was his cousin, only, "This is Francine."

He became The Man. On the football field he made touchdowns every game. Fans would yell, "Donkey! Donkey!" when he would run out onto the field.

But Don was not finished yet. He found that this was just too much fun. His finale came the last night of the football season.

The anthem had been sung, fans waited eagerly for the players to appear. Long moments passed and a hush came over the crowd. Where were the players? Still no sound. Then suddenly a loud braying was heard and out of the tunnel came Don Key riding a scarlet-coated donkey, and behind him came the players all braying and dancing a jig as they marched to their places.

The crowd went wild. Eric and Margaret, sitting in the stands looked at each other, and Margaret said, "You are right, my darling. Names do build character."

Eric replied, "Anon, it isn't over yet. You'll see."

*Allowed *Pensive *Elementary
*Hootenanny *Hoopla *Trample

MYSTERY OF LADY TRIUMPH

All the hoopla of the farmer's yearly Autumn Hootenanny was over.

The sign saying "NO UNAUTHORIZED FIREWORKS ALLOWED" sat askew on top of the large barn door that gaped open. The elementary school band had departed, and the square dancers were only a wraith of memory. The children hiding in the hayloft above had left, taking their secret spying and shocked sensibilities of adult behaviours with them. The ambulance was gone with the hysterical mother screeching to kingdom come because her two-year-old child had stuffed a cherry pit up her nose. A baby's bottle with the nipple half chewed by a dog lay next to a crumpled box of Cracker Jack. Beer bottles and cigarette butts lay scattered all over the wooden dance floor and the outside grassy area. A bewildered chicken came clucking out of a shipping crate.

Two men surveyed the shambles.

"Guess we gotta get to work," Jeff, the sturdy-looking workman, said. He was dressed in jeans and a worn denim jacket. He threw his cigarette butt down and stomped it into the dirt.

"Every year it gets worse, eh, Jeff?" said Crazy Pants.

Jeff looked at his old buddy and thought once again of how his loyal friend had come into his name. He glanced at his friend's rump where all the trouble had started. He had been pushed into a bonfire as a prank when they were kids, and his rump's muscle and fat had been burned away. From that time on, he had had to wear a soft pillow-sized padding sewn into his jeans by Molly Hart, the seamstress, so that he could sit down in comfort. Jeff shook away the memories and smiled at his friend.

Now it was time to clean up the remains. What Jeff and Crazy Pants never expected to find as they dug through the pile of debris were the remains of Letta Burrough's pet pig, Lady Triumph, named first-prize winner for the past five years running.

It was Jeff who made the gruesome discovery. He yelled, "What the hell!"

Crazy Pants ran across the lot. "Jeff, what's wrong?" He looked down and there at Jeff's feet was Lady Triumph. The huge first-prize blue ribbon, like a fine lady's hat, was stuck unto her head with a long skewer from the barbecue pit.

"It's Lady Triumph! Jeff, what we gonna do? Is she dead?"

"Of course she's dead, stupid. Some bastard shoved a skewer through her head."

"How long she's been gone, do ya think?"

"How do I know? I'm no doctor, but I know she was alive two hours ago," Jeff said. Head in hands, he sat down on the pile of tires that had been used for seating the crowd to watch the three-legged races. A long, pensive silence followed.

Crazy Pants left Jeff thinking. He walked around the lot mumbling his agitation, trampling the paper decorations that lay scattered about. "What the hell! What the hell!" he said over and over. "Who'd wanna kill Lady Triumph? The finest pig there ever was! Don't make no sense!"

Finally Jeff walked over to Crazy Pants. "I know who killed Lady Triumph. I figured it out, but I don't know what to do about it for sure. Still thinking on it. In the meantime, let's get her out of here. Get the wheelbarrow, and we'll load her onto my truck. The clean-up can wait till tomorrow.

Late that night, Jeff and Crazy Pants paid a visit to Neil MacAdams, who entered his pig, Westchester, every year and always came in second place. The rivalry was legend.

"We know you done it, Neil," said Crazy Pants.

"Done what, you retard?" Neil snarled and was about to slam the door.

Jeff put his foot in the doorway and pushed Neil inside. "Don't play innocent with us, Neil. We got proof!"

Neil's face flushed, and he stammered, "That's impossible; nobody was around."

When he realized his mistake, Neil said, "Now, my friends, my friends, don't do anything rash. I'd be in plenty of trouble if this should get out. What's your price for keeping it under your hats?"

"You know damn well that Letta Burrough is a special friend of ours, and you go and kill her prize possession. Lady Triumph was the best pig ever entered in the show, and you were so jealous that you had to put a skewer through her head. I'd like to put one through yours, you creep," Jeff said, as he grabbed Neil by the neck.

"Come on, Jeff, he's not worth it." Crazy Pants pulled Jeff away.

All three men stood staring at the floor and panting.

"If we go to the police, you're in big trouble, Neil," said Jeff

"I'll give you anything you want, only don't go there. How much to keep quiet? You guys, I've known you for ages. I made a big mistake letting my feelings get away from me. Please! Don't report me!"

Jeff and Crazy Pants looked at each other and both said, "We don't want your blood money!"

"Well, what do you want?"

Jeff was stumped. He could not think of a response.

It was Crazy Pants who finally said, "We want your silence, and your promise that you will never enter another pig in any contest again. Letta has one of Lady Triumph's litter that looks like a winner for next year. Lady Triumph's disappearance will forever remain a mystery. For this promise we will keep what we know to ourselves, right Jeff?"

"That's right!" Jeff said, relieved to have had the solution so ably handled by his friend.

In the truck going home Jeff said, "That was good thinking Crazy Pants. Only the three of us will ever know what happened to Lady Triumph and Neil sure as hell won't tell. So all's well that ends well, eh?"

"Not a bad solution for a 'retard', eh Jeff? Now let's get on with the butchering. There's enough pork there for all winter."

*Fluffy *Sincerity *Shelter
*Pathway *Voice *Corona

THE WIGGLE ROOM

I was next in line to enter the homeless shelter when a woman holding a little baby came up beside me. The guard at the door said, "No room left lady unless this young man will let you take his place."

I hadn't eaten all day, and I was soaked to the skin. The rain was still coming down in sheets. The water was dripping off the end of my nose like a leaky faucet, and my feet were sloshing in my decrepit runners. No way was I going to relinquish my chance of a shower, a hot meal, and a dry bed.

I shook my head. "No."

But then, I knew it was going to happen; I just knew it. I looked at the two of them. The baby was clutching what used to be a fluffy, plush rabbit. I could see it might have been white. Now, it was a soggy grey blob. Yet, the child snuggled it into his chest as if it were a glorious snippet of heaven itself. And the mother, oh, the mother! Eyes boring into mine with the pleading of the saints. I crumbled; I knew I would.

"Here lady," I said. Please take my place.

It always happened this way. I can no longer say no to the needy or the destitute.

You may think I am the needy and the destitute, but I can tell you right off that I am not. In all sincerity, I avow to you that I am wealthy for I have my innate element intact. What is poverty compared to the desolation of the soul?

I turned away into the night. There might be room for me in the stairwell of the parkade.

I wasn't always this wealthy. No, I was anything but. I drove a Rolls Royce, had a six-figure job, and lived in a penthouse overlooking the Inner Harbour. I was, what is termed by many, a "success". It all changed the night I met him.

I was sitting in the dimly lit corner of a bar one night after a very productive day of trading. I was smiling, smirking actually, thinking of the way I would beat out my stock market competitors the next day and make a haul; it promised to be over four million, free and clear. The insider tip I had received that afternoon was a sure thing.

I know now it was my greed that called him to me.

"Well, if it isn't Jerome! Mind if I join you?"

I looked up to see a tall, well-dressed man standing over me. His smile was genuine and his demeanour friendly.

"Do I know you?" I asked.

"Oh, I'm Mr. Corona. I have been watching how you work for a number of years. I may be able to help you do even better. Interested?" he asked.

"Always interested in doing better. Sit down, won't you?" I said.

I noticed his fingers were circled about with sparkling diamond rings. A gold stud was visible on the edge of his aquiline nose. He saw me also looking with fascination at his wrist.

"Ah," he said. "I see you have noticed my watch. It's a Chopard 201 Caret."

I couldn't believe what I was hearing. A Chopard 201, at $25 million dollars, is the most expensive watch in the world.

"Here," he said, "Try it on."

He handed it to me and went on to tell me what I was holding.

"You see there," he pointed, "a watch is buried beneath the rainbow of gems and precious stones, surrounded by three heart-shaped diamonds. Each is different from the other. The pink rock is fifteen carets, the blue is twelve carets, and the colourless rock is eleven carets. All these are fixed onto a diamond encrusted bracelet of white and yellow gold."

His dark eyes flashed as he spoke. His tongue was pierced with three gold studs. They glittered as he spoke. A quiver in his deep melodious voice sent shivers through me. He exuded admiration, bordering on love, for the expensive, beautiful jewellery he wore.

"It can all be yours, my friend. Let's get out of here. My car is waiting."

I felt compelled to join him. I wanted to see more of this man's prosperity, hoping I could luck into his strategy for reaching the pinnacle of affluence.

His chauffeur doffed his hat and opened the limo door for us. He received no direction from Mr. Corona but drove off without asking our destination. I got the distinct feeling he had driven this route many times before. A little flag waved in my brain, but I was too excited at the prospect of learning this man's secrets of success to pay attention to it.

After driving for an hour the evening light morphed into a night of total darkness. I was getting edgy and about to ask to be returned to the city. Just then, the limo turned into a long, curved driveway. Ahead was an enormous gabled structure with many windows. Every window exuded iridescent light that changed colours as we approached.

"Welcome to my residence, Jerome," Mr. Corona said as we came to a stop.

The chauffeur jumped out and opened the door for us.

"You will be glad you came, Jerome. I have so much to teach you."

We stepped onto a pathway of faintly lighted, glowing stones. I was not walking, for my feet were stationary. Yet I seemed to be moving along without conscious volition. Finally, we reached the door of this magnificent mansion.

The great oak portal opened when Mr. Corona said, "We are back, my splendid servant."

But when I looked about, there was no one in sight.

The great hall was lit with crystal chandeliers hanging from the high ceilings. Gilt-edged, old master paintings, which I did not recognize as having seen before in any collection, adorned the oaken walls. I was mesmerized by the opulence.

"Come this way, Jerome, to the teaching room."

He led me down a brightly lit corridor. I was aware of a coolness emanating from the walls as we walked, almost like the dampness of an abandoned well. I shook off the feeling of despondency that was wrapping around me. I looked back and saw that the corridor, which was well lit, had turned black behind each step we took. I hurried my steps into the light, but the dark shadow followed.

At last we reached a door, which opened once again, as Mr. Corona said, "We are back, my splendid servant."

The room, if it could be called a room, was a massive cave-like expanse, lit with glowing torches, which sputtered and blinked from their golden standards. The walls were studded with gemstones of every kind, shape, and colour. There was a glut of lavishness that somehow overpowered my senses.

In the centre of the space, a long table with silken coverings seemed to extend into infinity. It was laden with silver tureens filled with steaming bisques. Goat horn cornucopias spilled out fruits and vegetables of every variety; delectable delicacies placed on ornate, silver filigree patens abounded. Ornate golden chalices of wine, schooners of beer, goblets of liqueurs, and crystal bottles of brandy were visible as far as the eye could see. There were huge gold platters piled high with meats and fish of every description. Flowers from every pottage adorned the table and extended down the entire length, emitting a cloying, sweet scent.

I heard a clacking sound. I turned and saw that Mr. Corona was clicking his gold-studded tongue against his teeth. A string of saliva was hanging from his mouth. He was salivating like a hungry dog. When he caught my eye, he licked his lips and slurped the dribble back into his mouth. He smiled and said, "Is it not impressive, Jerome?"

I was slightly nauseated from the smells and scents and odours all mixed together, but I nodded and said, "Beyond impressive. Are we going to sample these delicacies?" I asked.

"I am shocked at your ignorance, my boy. If we eat them, they are gone. Try to understand, it is the possessing; yes, the possessing!" Mr. Corona crooned.

I was eager to get to the teaching room. It was not to be just yet for once again I was led to another amazing sight, a dais upon which rested a gilded throne.

Mr. Corona took his place on the throne. I stood beneath him. Suddenly my knees buckled and I was kneeling before him. I could not rise. He laughed aloud and said, "You can be sitting here one day, Jerome, instead of being a subservient member of the working class as you have hitherto been. This is your first motivation. Do you accept the dominion over lesser mortals?"

"I do," I responded, and once again, we were moving. The dais revolved, and we were in a musty room. Here the walls were lined with old mouldering books.

"These are the books from which I will teach you, Jerome," he said. "They hold the wisdom of the world, the art of acquiring wealth. The teachings are as old as time. All who learn from them will never want for any assets or possessions. The monetary stock of the world will be yours. Are you ready to start your lessons, Jerome?"

I was intoxicated with desire. I hungered to have these secrets revealed to me. Still I hesitated and said, "I've learned, Mr. Corona, that nothing comes for free. There is always a price attached. I know this with a surety, for I have had to fight tooth and nail for the status and position, which I now occupy. I'd be willing to close the deal with you if the terms are fair. What is the price tag here?"

He evaded my question and said, "Let me give you a sample lesson, Jerome.

"Here is the first concept: Flexibility in one's opinions and interpretations. There must always be room to manoeuvre. That includes people, beliefs, loyalties, and objects. It is simple; you just hold yourself to a standard of wishy-washy liberalism."

"Is this how you have amassed your fortune?" I asked.

"Oh, yes, yes, my son." He smiled and rubbed his diamond-studded hands together.

I was enthralled and transfixed by his words. But from somewhere deep within, a tiny voice whispered, "Enslavement is the price you will pay."

Suddenly, I was awakened to the horrifying prospect of bondage and servitude to the stone monolith of rapacity.

I cried out, "No, Mr. Corona, I am not willing to go forward with your instruction. I must leave now!"

Mr. Corona's face was bland, seemingly accepting of my decision, but then, ever so slowly, a subtle change came over him.

His fingers elongated and his nails became talons. His black hair parted above his forehead and out sprouted two little protuberances. His face hardened into a mask of sinister mien. It was a terrible face carved in quartz with glaring eyes of sapphire and long pointed teeth of gold, dripping with blood-red rubies.

"Be gone!" he bawled in a voice of thunder.

The walls were wiggling like snakes. The books slithered off the walls; the floor was shuddering. I found myself back in the dark corridor and felt my way along the writhing walls.

As I reached the exit hall, I heard his voice bellowing out a dictum:

"You who have once fondled the image
Of procurement beware
For enticement will ever be there –
Tempting you to return to me!"

The door hissed open, and I was free. I found myself taking great gasps of pure delicious air as I ran into the starless night. I was smitten with revulsion and contrition all at once.

Exhaustion overtook me and I fell helpless to the ground. The last thing I knew was that mother earth would sustain me and I was comforted.

Someone was shaking me. "Hey, bud, wake up! It's closing time. Pay your tab and be on your way. I'd say you've had enough for one night."

I jerked awake and found I was still sitting in the dimly lit corner of the bar.

If there is an epilogue then it is this: Shortly thereafter, I sold my assets and donated all the filthy lucre I had acquired to charity. I now live a life ordained by a force that speaks to my soul in a still, small voice.

I cannot refuse the outstretched hand. Nor can I ever forget that I was as near to spiritual extinction as a moth to a flame.

*Avenue *Window *Mirror
*Lemon *Ritual *Rat

FIFTY DOLLARS
WELL SPENT

It is afternoon, and I am rushing down the avenue trying to get out of the rain. I charge into a tiny, elderly Asian woman. I knock her down pretty hard. As I murmur an apology and pull her upright, she regains her footing and says, "Oh no, my fault, my fault." She hangs onto my arm and seems reluctant to let go.

"Are you hurt?" I ask.

"No, no, shaky, shaky."

"Well, I think we had better get out of this rain. How about I take you for a cup of tea?"

She smiles and nods.

We cross the street and enter an old restaurant. The hostess approaches, smiles, and asks, "Would you like to sit near the window, sir?"

"That would be fine." I don't know why I say that, for when I look at the window, I see heavy, sickly green drapery, hanging there like moss, hiding any view out the window. It is as if we are in a twilight zone, a weird sphere somewhere between the now and then. Only a dim light emanates from the small lamp on the table.

I pull out a chair and sit the fragile lady down. She smiles and sighs, and then proceeds to dig into her enormous handbag. What is she looking for I wonder. I do not have to wait long before she draws out a small, round mirror trimmed in gold. This she places before her on the table. Again she rummages in her bag and pulls out a crystal stone about the size and shape of a lemon. It is beautiful and as clear as fresh water reflecting rainbows. But she is not finished fishing in the bag. Out comes a worn leather-bound book. She lovingly places this on the table in front of her as well.

By this time I am wondering if she is right in the head. What is this cockeyed ritual? What have I let myself in for, and to tell the truth, I begin to sweat, just a little.

"What's all this?" I ask.

"You, you, are a rat!" she says with a toothy grin. "Yes, yes, I think so."

"Hey, lady, I said I was sorry for knocking you over and now you call me a rat? Just order your tea and something to go with it, please."

Again the little woman smiles. It is then I notice her gold front tooth that sparks when she smiles. The waitress comes to take our orders, and I am surprised when the woman orders a full course dinner not the tea we had come for.

"You not eating?" my little guest asks.

Well, I think, since *I've got to be here for the duration, I might as well have a meal too,* so I order the steak dinner as well.

"Good, good. Now we have time." She reaches over and touches my hand.

At the touch, my hand gets very hot and tingles, almost like an electric shock. I quickly pull it away and feel my face flush. This is getting weirder by the minute. I call the waitress over again and order a beer to calm my senses.

"Me too," the little crinkled creature says.

Time seems to not exist then. The beer comes, the meals come, and through all the chomping and sipping she talks and, wonder of wonders, so do I. It is as if a dam breaks inside of me. I tell her about my job cleaning at the medical centre, the way I am treated there by the doctors and nurses, who think I am beneath them.

She nods and murmurs her empathy. She talks of coming from Communist China and how hard it was when she lost her family during the Revolution. This hits me pretty hard for I know the pain of it, too – the emptiness and desolation, as if the world has become a desert. When tears come to her eyes and trickle down through the wrinkled cheeks, I cry too.

The waitress returns with the dessert menu.

"Banana cream pie very good, you too?" my companion asks.

I nod knowing there is no use in declining. When it arrives, we both dig in, smacking our lips and relishing the creamy goo. The sweetness somehow slides down to a place inside of me that is shielded, hidden for years from utterance and recognition. I feel it coming on... I blurt it out. I tell her something that I have never revealed to anyone.

"I hate myself! I'm a worthless cypher, good for squat! I've always dreamed of being a doctor, but what am I? I clean up the crap they leave behind, and they think I'm part of that crap!" I am breathing hard, trying to hold unto myself, shaking, wishing I could sink into the floor for what I have just disclosed.

Then, to my surprise, my companion calmly asks, "When were you born?"

I am stunned into a reply and I tell her: "February tenth, nineteen ninety-four."

"Yes, yes, you are a rat!" she squeals triumphantly. "A twenty-year-old rat."

There's that rat thing again, and I feel like a fool for what she has wormed out of me. But then she opens that dilapidated leather-bound book and says, "See, look here." She points to a page with a picture of a rat and some kind of queer writing. It finally hits me. She is referring to the Chinese Zodiac!

I start laughing, and she joins in. Now the tears running races down our cheeks are happy ones. She points again to the picture of the rat and then proceeds to tell me some very interesting things.

"There are good rats and bad rats. You are Mr. Good Rat, but you use bad qualities of rat, like self-destructive and vindictive. These, they bad, hold you back. You must use good qualities like industry, tenacious, hard work. You are sensitive, Mr. Good Rat. You only twenty. You study hard and become Doctor Good Rat. Okay?"

She laughs aloud, her gold tooth sparks, and I feel like I may be worth something after all. Dr. Good Rat. Hah! But it's not over. She hands me that crystal and says, "Hold it over heart." I do and a great rush of warmth explodes in my chest. I have never felt anything like it. A calmness envelopes me, and I feel like I am being rocked to sleep in a cozy hammock on a balmy summer's day.

She says, "Mr. Good Rat, please you keep crystal and use to make you better."

"Thank you, thank you," is all I can muster.

My little lady tucks the book back in her bag just as the waitress comes with the bill.

I help the lady up from her chair and then go to the front desk and haul out my credit card. She follows behind me.

"Wait just a minute," I say to her.

Wow, I think, *fifty dollars plus a tip!* But it is the best fifty I have ever spent.

Finally, I turn around to her, but she is not there. A little panic starts to build. "Did you see her?" I ask the waitress.

"Yeah," she left.

I rush out the door onto the rain-soaked street. It is now evening. We must have talked for hours. I start to call out and then realize I don't even know her name. There is no one in sight.

She, my little enigmatic wizard, is gone. A sigh of disappointment starting at my feet rises into my head, and I feel a great loneliness like when I lost my folks so many years ago.

Suddenly, I hear a voice calling. "Sir, sir, you forgot something." It is the waitress. She hands me the little gold-rimmed mirror that my lady must have left on the table.

"Thanks," I say. I hold the mirror up in front of my face. The glow from the streetlight makes it possible to just discern an image. I swear it is the wrinkled little puss, smiling, gold tooth twinkling, looking back at me. I carefully put the treasured item in my pocket along with the healing crystal.

I turn and start walking home, knowing that what has happened is not happenstance. The rain drizzles down, but I do not mind. I have plans to make. A smile tickles the edges of my mouth and then a roar of laughter bursts out of me. I shout to the night: "Dr. Good Rat! That's me!"

*Gregarious * Listening *Socks
Beleaguered Nefarious *Tears

THE LISTENING RAVENS

Albert Stargazer is my real name, but the other boys in the group home call me Crapper. I guess I brought this on myself because I told them the story of how the Blackfoot got horses. It goes like this:

"There are two orphan children. The sister is adopted, but the boy – who is deaf and seems stupid – is scorned and abandoned by the tribe. He follows the tribe and gets his hearing back. He is then adopted by a kind, old chief – Good Running – who takes pity on him. The boy wants to do something great, and Good Running reluctantly suggests that he could try to fetch back Elk Dogs (which are horses) for the tribe. No one else has ever succeeded.

The boy meets a man at a pond, who says he can't help, and then a monstrous man at a lake, who says likewise. Finally, he meets a dazzlingly dressed boy by a lake, who offers to take him to meet his grandfather beneath the lake. Bravely, the orphan boy plunges in after his guide and finds he can breathe and does not get wet. He is shown how to ride Elk Dogs, and by glimpsing the grandfather's feet (which are hooves), he earns three wishes. He takes the old man's magical belt and robe and half of the Elk Dogs back to his tribe. This is how the Blackfoot got horses."

The boys yelled, "What a load of crap." Now I'm known as Crapper.

The strange thing is though, that almost every night they come into my room and get me to tell them another story by taunting me and saying, "Hey, Crapper, we know you haven't got it in you to tell another far-fetched story. You're all crapped out."

I fall for it every time. I can't help myself. The stories just fill my brain and out they come. After they all leave, Socks comes into my room and cuddles down next to me. I hide him under the covers because the guys are always teasing him.

I love that cat. He's glacier white with black speckled paws, like salt and pepper. That's why I call him "Socks". Everyone else just calls him "Cat". Whenever the guys try to rough him up, he hides. Only I know where. He hides in full view by straddling the top of the open door to the rec room. He just hangs there, safe, because nobody ever looks up. Even on the street, I never see anybody look up to the ever-changing sky. My poor beleaguered Socks. I pretend I can't see him so as not to give away his secret hiding place. It would be a calamity and a breach of trust if I did.

You might wonder what I am doing in this place. I've been here for four years. I came when I was fourteen. Tomorrow, I have to leave. The social worker has found me a place where he thinks I will be happy. It's out of the city on an estate where I will be helping the gardener with landscaping and upkeep. He said I will have my own digs above a garage. Only thing is, I will miss Socks. They say he isn't my cat, but he knows he is and so do I.

So, tonight I am talking to the Listening Ravens of All Knowingness, telling them all about what's going to happen. They know all about why I am here in the first place. I heard the social worker say it four years ago when they took me from the reservation because of my father's nefarious actions and neglect of me. They said that I'm an autistic savant, but a rather gregarious boy. A few years ago, I would have been known as an idiot savant. I remember everything and every word I read and whatever words I hear. Even all the words in my head that I have to let out.

Like the time my father and I were out hunting for the birds that my father sold illegally to a taxidermist in the city. I hated having to find and carry the birds my father shot with an arrow.

"It's the best way, no noise. Nobody needs to know, you understand idiot boy?" he had said.

We lived in a shack on the edge of the reservation. Nobody much ever came to visit us. My father went out every night. I don't know where, but he would come home late at night and curse and holler at the moon and stars.

I would call in the centre of my dream mind to the Listening Ravens and they answered me with the wisdom of silence. I would take their advice, and I was mostly silent. I would say verses from the Bible into my pillow, over and over. My favourite was Jude 13:31. "Raging waves of the sea, foaming out their own shame. Wandering stars, to whom is reserved the blackness of darkness forever."

On the last morning that I went with my father to kill beautiful birds I knew I couldn't pick them up anymore – none of them and especially that eagle. The arrow brought it down, and my father said, "Go fetch it."

I found the eagle struggling in tall river reeds. The magnificent bird lay wet and bloody, still convulsing. I removed the shaft in one quick pull. A twist of the neck and the eagle lay still. I straightened its wings and smoothed its feathers. Then lifting it gently, I waded out to where the current ran. I placed it on the sparkling water. Slowly round it floated once. Drops like red tears tinged the water, and then the river swept it away. A cloud drifted across the sun, and I felt a chill run through me.

"Goodbye, my brother," I whispered.

Then I felt a rage within me like a boiling pot about to run over.

I returned to where my father stood, further up the bank. He growled, "You were gone so long. Where's the eagle? Did you find it?"

"No."

"Stupid idiot! That will lose me a fortune! You bloody imbecile!"

All the time he was beating me I sang, "Alleluia, Alleluia," louder and louder, until I could hear the clouds singing and the wind whistling and the trees clapping.

That night, the RCMP came and took him away and took me away, and here I am, and tomorrow the social worker will take me away again to my new home.

It's early, 6:00 a.m.; the social worker is coming at 7:00. I need to finish stuffing my belongings into the old duffle bag I brought with me four years ago. I am strangely disconnected this morning. I didn't say goodbye to the guys last night, and now I can't find Socks. It's just as well, I guess, because I might break down and cry, and a man of eighteen doesn't cry, I've heard.

Here's the social worker. We are off.

Two hours later, and I am meeting Mr. Earnshaw, the gardener, and his wife, Mrs. Earnshaw. "Call me Jack, and my wife is Millie. After you get settled, come on over for a chat and a cup of coffee, Albert."

My face is on fire. I feel like jumping up and down. He called me Albert!

Wow, these rooms above the garage have everything: a TV, a desk and bookshelves, a double bed with sheets and blankets, a kitchen, a bathtub and shower, all my own. There are windows that look out at the gardens and sky and even a dartboard! It's like I've been transplanted into heaven.

As I unpack my duffle bag, I hear a muffled cry. I go to the window, but see nothing down below. Again, I hear it but cannot place where the sound is coming from. As I dig out an old sweater and jeans from the duffel bag, I feel something soft. A low murmur. A speckled paw grabs at my hand.

I hold Socks in my arms and kneel to thank the Listening Ravens. My friend licks the tears that are running down my face. So much for being a man of eighteen.

*Eclipse *Mayhem *Mystery
*Psyche *Covert *Imbecile

THE INTERVIEW

There was nothing about him that would have drawn attention from the casual observer. He was just an old man, part of the silent majority, bent almost in half with arthritis. It was only when, in close proximity, that the full impact hit. This is when his eyes, the colour of slate, bore into mine. I was mesmerized, caught like a thief in the glare of a police takedown light. All the polish came off, and I was exposed. He could see right through me to my inner core.

Somewhere deep inside, the warning nudge came for me, but I ignored it. My gut feeling was eclipsed by curiosity. I was riveted to the spot. Right there, that minute, my life derailed, and I was caught in a monstrous maze of mayhem and mystery.

It all began when I answered the ad for a position as a ghostwriter and companion-helper-cook for a disabled gentleman. It was a strange combination, but hey, I needed something different. I was tired and frustrated with the daily grind down at the newspaper office. With my impressive resume I knew I would get the job, hands down. I had all the prerequisite qualifications. I was a damn good writer and one hell of a cook. I had had a long period of prosperity as the star journalist for The Comet, but the grind had worn me down. I needed a change, and I thought this would be just the cure, a kind of rest period.

I never had an inkling of how the lovely chords of my life's music would morph into a discordant, off-key jangle of intrigue and subterfuge. As a journalist I often used subterfuge to get the story, but this time, the tables would be turned, and I would be the one caught in the smokescreen of a cunning dismemberment of my psyche.

I arrived a few minutes early for the interview, checking myself in the car's sunscreen mirror to make sure my hair stayed down, and then I pulled up to the iron gate. It opened. *Automatic sensor*, I thought. Good, I was expected.

I drove down the long driveway and was amazed to see the palatial house, so out of place, set back from the busy road of the dilapidated neighbourhood through which I had driven on my way here.

Two huge, stone rottweiler dogs sat on either side of the heavy oak door. I stood there wondering if I had made a mistake in coming, for I had a chill run through me like icy sleet. It was then that I noticed the tiny camera placed just above the door. Again, I felt the strange premonition, that signal in the gut that says "be wary", but the self-willed guy that I am thought, *I've come this far; might as well go all the way.* I pressed the door button and heard a bell peal and the sound of barking deep within the house.

It was a long wait for someone to come, so I had a chance to turn around and view the park-like gardens. I marvelled at the tranquillity of the scene; it was in bizarre conflict with what was in the neighbourhood beyond the gate.

Finally, the door opened, and I was greeted by a butler, who seemed to have stepped out of the last century. He was stiff and officious. He greeted me by name and said, "Follow me, sir. The master is expecting you."

I followed him down a long hall, our footsteps echoing hollowly on the hard parquet floor. The walls were lined with paintings, and they looked like old master originals. There was a huge crucifix at the end of the hall lit by covert lighting. I felt as if I were in a monastery and must tread softly.

We reached the end of the hall and turned right into a dimly lit study. Three walls were lined with books from floor to ceiling.

A voice quavered, "Thank you, Hans. We will have coffee and brandy in thirty minutes."

I wanted to say that I don't drink brandy, but the voice came again saying, "Have a seat Mr. Abrams. Make yourself comfortable. Would you like a cigarette?"

I looked over, and there behind a huge mahogany desk sat the man who would haunt me for the rest of my life.

He repeated, "A cigarette?"

"No, thank you."

"A cigar then. Cuban?"

Again, I declined and felt those dissecting eyes peering into mine.

"If I offered you a toke would that be more to your liking?"

What's he talking about? I thought, but before I could reply, he smiled and slid his hand over the desk as if wiping away his last sly comment.

He reached over to a drawer on his left and pulled out my letter and my resume. He began reading it aloud.

"It says here in your letter of introduction that your superior says you are a star reporter. Do you believe that if you have a superior that you are somehow inferior?"

I am shocked and put off by the question. "Not at all."

But before I can go on, he interrupts and says, "So you believe then that all men are equal."

"Well, yes I do, in many respects. That is, all men are unique and have special talents."

"Even the imbecile or the crippled?"

Where the hell is this going? I think, but once again he interrupts and makes what sounds like a purposeful statement.

"It says here in your letter that you are a star reporter."

I nod and think that maybe now we will get down to the reason I am here but no. There he goes again.

"A star. Very interesting choice of words, do you not think so, Mr. Abrams? This suggests that you are above others, wouldn't you say?"

My gut is wrenching and I feel anger building.

"Where are you from Mr. Abrams?"

"I'm Canadian, born right here in Montreal."

"No, I mean what is your ancestry?"

"My ancestry? Why is that pertinent to this interview?"

"I am asking the questions, Mr. Abrams. Perhaps you are not proud of where you spring from? What tribe would that be now? I stand up and lean over the desk. "I think I have made a mistake in coming here." My face is inches away from his, and I see the sag and droop. The lines of derision deeply etched into his pale skin.

"Oh, sit down, Mr. Abrams. You have to allow this old man his silly follies. Let's get down to the details of what I need in an employee. As it said in the advertisement, I need a ghostwriter who can keep his mouth shut and write my story as I tell it. Of course, it will not be published until after my demise. I think you could do that. Oh yes, and a cook. I need a cook. Simple food. Yes simple. It doesn't have to be kosher, you know."

My stomach is churning, and I have to swallow the bile that fills my throat. I am looking at a monster.

I am up and walking to the door when I hear his high-pitched squeal of a laugh. Then he is shouting, "You are all the same, thinking you are equal! Never, never, you Christ killers!"

A cyclone of emotions propels me out onto the driveway. I jump into my car and cushion my head in my hands. I am shaking so badly that I cannot put the key into the ignition. Tears pour from my eyes as I remember my grandmother's night-long laments as she recalled the horrors of the camps. Finally, I am speeding down the driveway out onto the dilapidated street. I take no notice of the uneven pavement, nor the stench of decay filtering through the air.

It has been two months since that day. I have still not returned to *The Comet*. I told them I am on a sabbatical. Tomorrow, I leave for Israel. Someday perhaps I will have the courage to fight the stagnant hate, but for now, I will go home to learn more of my proud heritage.

Tonight, I travel down that road of ruin to view for the final time the place where I came to know myself. Where prejudice spewed its rancid juice into my psyche. "Two thousand sixteen and still it lives," I say aloud in awe at the realization.

I slow down where the gate had been, but there is no entrance. I drive up and down that street over ten times, but still I cannot find the property. It seems to have disappeared, faded, but I know in my heart that the pale horse will have many riders once again.

*Tremble *Garden *Undercurrent
*Psychic *Façade *Soirees

THE LAVENDER FIELD

There was something elusive, lurking, and trembling at the edge of naming that pricked at her mind every time Georgina saw them together.

It wasn't that they weren't a handsome-looking couple. They were. It wasn't that their elderly neighbours in the expensive, gated retirement community did not hold them in the highest esteem. They did. It wasn't the cuteness of the nicknames this Russian couple had for each other. He was Sputnik; she was Sweet Grass. They were generous. *Had they not invited the entire community to their sumptuous fortieth wedding anniversary party just last week? Did they not share the luxuriant lavender that grew like a great blue-mauve coloured tapestry in their extensive back garden? Do I not have some of their sweet-smelling, dried lavender in little pouches in my lingerie drawer? I do.*

These were the thoughts that coursed through her mind like a slow-moving river. She couldn't realize the dangerous undercurrents therein. It wasn't any of this that tilted her usual acceptance of anyone at face value. But her psychic antennae was up and would not let her rest until she satisfied the nagging suspicion that these two were not really who they portrayed. They were too perfect.

She should have left well enough alone, but her inquisitive nature would not let her. There was definitely something not right about Sputnik and

Sweet Grass. And Georgina had to know what lay beneath their façade. It was as if a dark pool of stagnant water breeding mosquitoes was beckoning her.

So it was that Georgina inserted herself like a subtle question mark into the lives of Sputnik and Sweet Grass. She thought she was being very adroit and skilful with her sly, prying ways.

It was at the boisterous pool party that Georgina approached Sweet Grass. Using her most piteous voice, she said, "Oh, how I wish my Edward were still here. I know he would love to have met you and your husband. It gets pretty lonely at times without him to talk to."

Sweet Grass looked at her with empathetic eyes. "It must be very difficult, Georgina. But you can call on us any time you are feeling low."

"How kind you are. I wouldn't want to impose." Georgina looked down at her sandaled feet, not wanting Sweet Grass to see her look of triumph.

Hah! I've got my in, Georgina thought.

It didn't happen right away, but within six weeks, Georgina had wormed her way into the inner sanctum of the Russian couple's life. She was invited to all of their soirees.

One night after all the guests had left, Georgina lingered and offered to help tidy up.

"Oh, thank you, Georgina. I do appreciate your offer, but we have a maid that comes in every day. Come and sit awhile with Sputnik and me. Have a final nightcap."

Georgina had watched the couple all evening drinking White Russians. They had fallen in love with the American drink. Now they sat together on the sofa dreamily looking at Georgina.

Georgina asked, "How did you come to nickname each other Sputnik and Sweet Grass?"

"Of course, you know about Sputnik. It was the first artificial Earth satellite. It was visible all around the earth. It shows Russian superiority," Sputnik said.

"That's my Sputnik! Known all over the world," Sweet Grass said drunkenly.

"I call my wife 'Sweet Grass' because in the Russian Steppe, the grass grows tall and sweet and strong. This is my Sweet Grass," he murmured. Sputnik was almost asleep.

"I must be off," Georgina said.

As she left, she wondered how this couple could have saved enough money in their ten years in the country to afford their opulent furnishings and lifestyle.

Early the next morning, Sputnik phoned Georgina and asked if she could come and stay with Sweet Grass, as she was ill.

"She won't go to the doctor, but I have asked him to make a house call. I have been called out of town on an emergency. I will be gone for two days. Your help is much appreciated," he said.

Georgina was happy to do this, as she wanted to feel out Sweet Grass as to how they had acquired their wealth. When she arrived, the doctor was there.

"Please just be here when Sweet Grass wakes up. I've given her a sleeping potion. She was in a lot of pain. It's her back. It goes out periodically, and she can't move for days. She'll be out for at least four hours. Thank you for your kindness in being here for her," the doctor said.

Georgina smiled and nodded. "It's my pleasure to help," she said.

When the maid came, Georgina dismissed her, saying she wasn't needed. Georgina cleaned up the party mess of the night before and then went to check on Sweet Grass. Sweet Grass was sleeping soundly.

Georgina went downstairs to the study. "Here's where I'll find my answers," she mumbled to herself.

She pried open locked drawers until she came upon something that sparked her interest. There were many correspondences with the initials GH. "What does this mean?" she asked herself. Finally she found the mother lode on the computer. She entered the initials GH. What came up startled her, and she knew she had her answer.

"Oh, my God!" she cried aloud. There it was. Sputnik was the drug lord known as the Goliath Heron. She had read about him, named after the goliath heron with a huge wingspan of seven feet. *How apt a name for him,* she thought.

But now that her curiosity was satisfied, she knew she must report her findings to the police. Then another thought snaked through her mind.

When Sweet Grass finally awoke, Georgina brought her toast and a cup of tea. She sat herself on the edge of the bed, leaned close to Sweet Grass, and whispered, "Have you ever heard of the great goliath heron? It must be a magnificent bird. I read somewhere that it has a wingspan of seven feet."

Sweet Grass gasped and turned pale. "What do you want Georgina?" she asked in a low, barely discernable murmur.

"Let's discuss it when GH gets back, shall we? In the meantime, I promised your husband that I would look after you. It will only be a few days until he returns from his business trip." Georgina sneered the word "business" and patted Sweet Grass.

The meeting took place two days later when Sputnik returned.

When the moving truck came to clear out Georgina's house, the neighbours were saddened to learn that Georgina had moved to Florida on a whim.

"She didn't even say goodbye. How rude!" they said and promptly forgot all about her.

A few nights later, Sputnik and Sweet Grass sat drinking White Russians. Sputnik stood up and stretched his back. He pulled Sweet Grass up into his arms.

"That was a close call, Sweet Grass," he said.

"Never mind, my darling Sputnik, the lavender will smell much sweeter next spring," she said.

"Yes, the fertilizer will do wonders," he replied.

Sputnik and Sweet Grass looked at each other and laughed uproariously. They were holding each other up, shaking with uncontrolled mirth at their droll sense of humour.

A neighbour walking by their home with his dog Max heard the laughter and saw Sputnik and Sweet Grass through the wide living-room window.

He said aloud, with a touch of envy, "That sweet, jolly couple, always happy! We really should get to know them better, eh Max?"

*Antipathy *Tornado *Sidewalk
*Sunny *Moon bow

I'LL TELL YOU TOMORROW

There was no antipathy in him. He saw the wonder in everything, especially the wind. He said the wind talked to him. He called the wind Ajax. He was nature's child and that is why we called him Sunny and that is also why he is no longer with us.

When he was six years old and just starting school, he came home ecstatic as he described little desks lined up like box-cars on a train. He said, "I was in the front, so I told the kids that I am the engineer. The teacher said we aren't supposed to talk out loud, but I can whisper to myself and the wind, and that teacher will never know what I say or what the wind answers back to me."

"What do you say to yourself? And what does the wind tell you?" my husband and I asked.

He grinned and said, "I'll tell you tomorrow."

This became his mantra and stock answer to many questions that we put to him over the years. He wasn't secretive. He just held his joy tight within himself.

I remember on one occasion we had to pry an answer out of him. He was seven years old, and he was inconsolable one night as we tucked him into bed. He clung to me and cried.

"What is it, Sunny?" we asked over and over again.

Finally, weeping uncontrollably, he said, "I'm sorry mama. Today I stepped on a crack on the sidewalk, and now you will have a broken back!"

He was, even as a young man, gullible and naïve. It was his trusting, non-suspicious nature that disarmed all who came in contact with him.

One autumn night, there was a terrific windstorm that uprooted trees and even blew them away. We had a hundred-year-old ash tree in our garden that was wrenched from the ground and landed in the street. The next morning, we could not find Sunny. His bed had not been slept in. We ran out into the garden.

"Sunny, Sunny," we called. "Where are you?"

We heard him laughing. Then his head popped out of the depression where the ash tree's roots had been. It had filled with colourful leaves during the storm, and he had made his bed there.

"Mom, you should have heard what the wind told me last night!" he looked ecstatic.

"What did the wind tell you, Sunny?"

But once again the answer was the same.

"I'll tell you tomorrow."

During his secondary school years he reiterated again and again that, "Wind power holds supremacy over all the natural elements."

So, we were not surprised when, after he graduated from high school, he decided to study Wind Science at university. His doctoral thesis won international acclaim. This enabled him to be hired by a leading laboratory and wind turbine exploration firm.

One day, a few months after his initial employment, he came to us and said, "Mom and Dad, I will be doing more research on tornados. You've heard of storm- chasers haven't you?"

"Won't that be dangerous son? Is this part of your new job?"

"No, not really, but my friend and I want to be there to capture the reality and beauty of it all. Bill is a great photographer and has a truck outfitted with all we need to get some great shots and information. I think this will further my work."

I grabbed my husband's hand when I heard these plans. My husband frowned and said, "Sunny, maybe this is going a bit too far."

"Oh, no Dad, it will be fine. Bill and I know what we are doing. Don't be worrywarts. When has the wind ever been my enemy?"

And so it was…

Three summers later, Bill was at our door, trying to explain what had happened.

"We were chasing the tornado. It was a fierce one, but the shots were great and all the instruments were working fine. Suddenly, the monster turned on us. Sunny yelled, "There's a deep culvert on the side of the road. Let's make a run for it!"

I dove into the culvert thinking Sunny was right behind me, but when I looked back, he just wasn't there. The truck was gone. Sunny was gone!"

Bill was weeping. My husband and I held him and murmured, "It's not your fault. It's not your fault."

Our hearts were broken too.

Twenty years have passed, and our hearts are still fragmented. We do not know where Sunny is. The wind took him away.

Last night I had a dream. I saw Sunny. It was night. He was smiling and gazing at a sparkling waterfall with a moon bow arching over it. The colours were magnificent as was my Sunny. He turned to me and I saw his dark hair moving in a slight breeze.

I called out, "Sunny, what is this place? Where are you?"

He smiled and said mischievously, "Mama, you know. I'll tell you tomorrow!"

When I told my husband of the dream, he held me and whispered, "Tomorrow is only a day away for us now, my love."

*Ridiculous *Excelsior *Morgue
*Karma *Surroundings *Silver

SOMETHING TO
BELIEVE IN

Before she kicked his wheelchair down the stairs, she kissed him goodbye. He didn't know it would be the last slushy lip-to-lip, tongue-to-tongue contact that he had insisted on and so relished over the years. The long, long ten years.

"Free at last," she sighed.

She smiled as she dialled 911. She then drew a great breath and screamed into the phone, "Oh, my God, my husband has fallen down the stairs!"

The explanation to the police held water, it seemed, for they nodded in sympathy as she told the story. "I heard him shout and then a loud banging. I was just getting up myself. I have no idea how he went down the stairs in his wheelchair. He must have been disoriented. He always takes the elevator down for breakfast." Her tears were as dry as grains of uncooked rice as she tried to squeeze them into the hankie she held to her eyes.

Twelve months later, after the inquest was over and the life insurance investigation was settled, Margot put the mansion up for sale. She sold all the furniture and paintings at auction. Her net worth was now well over a billion dollars.

"On this auspicious occasion, let us raise our glasses to my new life. I will never have to work again," she told her girlfriend, Becky, at the swanky Excelsior Bar, where the posh surroundings fit in perfectly with her new moneyed status.

"You call living in luxury for ten years "work"?" Becky said with a laugh.

"Yeah, I do." Margo fidgeted and twisted her silver necklace with the inset emeralds around her fingers. She grimaced. "It was a twenty-four-seven job, I tell you."

"That's ridiculous! All you had to do was humour the old boy."

"It was the toughest job I ever had. I thought when I married him at his age of eighty-seven that I would be free in a couple of years at most, but come on, Becky, you know he just went on and on for ten years. That's what I call work! And I never want to see the inside of a morgue again, that's for damn sure. They made me see him there. It was freaky."

"Yeah, I suppose it was. What about that son of his, Richard? What did he get?"

"Almost nothing. I was able to hire the best lawyers. Oh, Richard was pissed alright, but I'm the one who put up with the old codger all those years, wasn't I?"

"Well, you still look pretty good for forty. Something will come up for you, I'm sure."

Both women laughed uproariously at the unintentional, pervy remark.

"Let's get out of here," Margot said. "I've got a hair appointment."

Her limo driver smiled as he held the door open for the women. He didn't smile when he cruised through a red light and was crushed by a semi. Becky died at the scene too. Margot was rushed to emergency in critical condition.

Six months later she got the news.

"You will never regain the use of your legs. Paralysis is permanent, I am afraid," the kindly doctor announced.

Later that day, before the shock of the pronouncement's weeping jag was over, the nurse said, "You have a visitor, Margot." She arranged the flowers on the table beside Margot's wheelchair and stared at the handsome man who stood in the doorway.

Margot gulped down her tears, looked up, and when she saw who her visitor was, she blanched and sobbed, "Oh, Richard, I am so sorry for everything. I did love your father, you know. Really I did."

"You pitiful excuse for a human being. I just came by to see for myself. I heard you were in an accident and would never walk again. It gives me no satisfaction to see you like this." Richard turned away.

As he left the room, he heard Margot cry out, "Richard, don't leave me like this. I'm desolate. Please, give me something to believe in!"

Richard paused and, without turning, whispered, "Karma! Believe in that!"

*Prairie *Storm *Coma *Heartbeat
*Valley *Laughter

THE GHOST CHAIR

"Come on, Roger. Buddy, wake up!"

It's Bill again, telling me to wake up. I hear him clear as day. His voice filters through the scene that plays over and over before me, but I just sit here, wherever here is.

I watch without emotion as if all that happened is a dream.

Bill and I are driving home. Another day spent servicing the turbines. As I drive, I watch the wind turbines and think they look like black skeletons doing calisthenics on the bluff overlooking the river. Soon a flotilla of dark grey clouds speeds across the endless expanse of prairie sky. There is a flash and thundering as the battalion gathers the elements to storm the earth.

A sheet of rain as dense as a final curtain, falls. Oncoming headlights are barely discernible. Suddenly bullets of hail shatter the windshield of our truck, glass everywhere. I can't see.

Bill shouting, "Roger, a semi ahead. Brake! Brake!"

Another voice, soft like marshmallow. It's Ma. "Hello Bill. Any change?"

"No, I'm afraid not, Mrs. Haley. Doc says sometimes these comas can last a long time."

"It has already been a year. My poor son, will he ever wake up?"

"I hope so, Mrs. Haley. I hope so."

"You have been so faithful, Bill. Coming to see Roger every day. Thank you."

"I'll keep coming too. I know he can hear me. I just know it."

"Oh, my poor boy. I kiss him and hold his hand, but there is no response."

There is a catch in Ma's voice that tugs at me and something changes. I begin to notice where I am. I am sitting on a chair made of white vapour it seems. I am also weightless, but now I desperately want to grab Ma's hand and never let go. With all my might I try to move my hand. I want to tell Bill I'm okay. Nothing happens.

There are alarms going off. What's going on I wonder?

Bill is calling, "Stay with me, Roger. Stay with me."

Other voices, "That was close ... cardiac arrest ... stable now."

I smell the rain. It is falling all around me, but I am dry. I watch a flower drinking the soft drops. I hear water gurgling with laughter as it runs down the drainpipe into Papa's rain barrel.

Bill is here.

"Hey buddy, how's it going? You sure gave us a scare. You gotta stick around, Roger. There's a lotta living yet to do, old man. I'll be back in the morning."

I am watching a bumblebee wake up. Its bed is a leaf. First it stretches one leg, then the other. I can almost hear it yawn. It opens its eyes. After a slight pause it flies away.

There is a new feeling here. I can see further, a valley, and beyond it the ocean, ebbing and flowing, ebbing and flowing like a heartbeat.

Bill is here.

"Roger, I have news. Remember Sofia? Well, we're getting married next month. I sure would like you to be my best man. You are my best man even so. Try my brother; try to be there. Wake up, Roger, please."

I haven't heard Bill cry since we were kids, when his dog Puck was hit by a car. This is different though, not a hysterical wailing, more like a deep digging down to a place where sorrow lives.

My chair seems to be tipping. I clutch onto nothing and right myself. The sky looks to be tilted. It is interesting and I am not afraid. Ma is smiling and holding a baby boy named Roger. There is a dim light far off.

There is whispered conversation in the hall.

Bill is here.

"Dear old buddy, Doc says you won't be making it. All I can say is, 'Safe journey. You are free.'"

A surge of happiness runs through me. Drawing in a deep breath of gratitude, I look toward the light, brighter now than a thousand headlights. There is the scent of prairie grasses, a remembrance so deep and soul wrenching that a flood of joyful tears breaks from me. I am home, for home is where my story began.

*Paper flower *Glacier *Compatriot
*Mindless *Crinkle *Planet

PAPER FLOWERS FOR PAPA

I want to scream, "Papa, don't go!" But it is no use. He is receding like a blue-ice glacier. Drop by drop, his essence is melting into the cold lake of another dimension, feeding a river that flows endlessly to the sea.

Papa loved words, and although he had no formal education, he always said, "Books are for learning, so read them, Tomaso."

His favourite word was "compatriot". He thought this word best described his relationship with his old cronies, who had come through a World War in Italy and then immigrated to Canada together. He said that the prefix "com" means "together", and a "patriot" is one who is willing to defend their country or friends against enemies or detractors. Papa told me that this is what he and his friends did in Italy and here in Canada.

His face would crinkle like cellophane when he laughed. How will I survive without him? Even though I am away at university, I always knew he was there. Now that I am back I cannot stay in the house. It is an empty shell without him. I have a room at the hotel.

I remember how we would sit in the middle of the meadow and gaze up at the stars on a dark, quiet night when all was still. "This is the time to talk to God, tell him your troubles, ask your questions when all is quiet. Then you can hear his answers," he would say.

Tonight, I am in the house, looking around, remembering, talking to God, asking why my papa has to go, but I receive no reply. I look over to where we used to sit to study Italian. The crumpled, brown leather sofa still looks inviting, but I cannot bear to sit on it. I would be swallowed in its shelter and never leave.

I must return to the hospital.

As I turn to leave the living room, I glimpse something on the fireplace mantel. An old crockery jar rammed full of paper flowers that I made when I was ten and learning origami at school. Tears pop from my eyes. Why did he keep them all these years?

I sob when the answer comes. He loves me. He will always love me. A certain comfort fills me and a firm strength rises in me. He needs me to be strong now, more than ever before.

When I return to the hospital, I hold his hand. He opens his eyes and whispers, "Tomaso, did you get your answer?"

"Yes, Papa," I reply.

His spark is draining away like a leaking battery, and soon there will be no life left, leaving me to knit together a life without him.

Suddenly, there is silence. The silence that signals the transformation, the great divide. I run my hand over his eyelids. "Be off now, Papa." He has gone, but not far, for I feel him in every molecule within me.

The night before the funeral a lightning storm raced through the town. The old oak tree in the front yard was struck, and it toppled onto the weathered frame structure. Electrical wires were severed, setting off a blaze that was seen all over town. The house went up in flames. By morning, nothing was left but a pile of smouldering rubble. Nothing.

I have graduated this spring. It has been two years since I last visited the cemetery. It is lush and green; colourful wild flowers bloom between the graves. There are others here searching too. I wander between the headstones looking for his. I hear him just as plainly as if he stands before me. "Tomaso, don't be like some of these mindless folks, be purpose-driven. Find out what you must do to be worthy of taking up space on this planet."

I think back to our years together and know that I was his purpose. "I won't fail you," I say aloud.

Just before I get to Papa's grave, I hear some stranger ask, "What's on that grave?"

Another replies, "Looks like someone's idea of a joke. Imagine putting paper flowers on a grave! Who would do such a thing?"

I smile and whisper, "Papa."

*Crimson *Argument *Submissive
*Urn *Tame *Crow

TOO LATE

Daybreak was having an argument with the elements. Fingers of crimson light stretched across the horizon, promising sunrise, while dark angry clouds gathered in the West threatening snow. The temperature had fallen rapidly, and the wet highway would soon turn to ice. I had a five-hour drive ahead of me.

I could not be late for the symposium on solar energy. I was one of the speakers. I had submitted a paper decrying the use of nuclear power, and this morning I would have to defend my position. This was my one big chance for worldwide recognition. I had already received accolades from some of the world's finest scientists. This talk would cement my position.

I had wanted to get an early start, but just as I was about to leave my hotel room, there was an emergency phone call from my six-year-old son. His tame crow, Lexi, had laid two eggs, and as my son picked one up, he dropped it.

"What kind of a daddy am I?" he sobbed. I promised Lexi I would always look after her, and now I've killed her baby!"

I tried reasoning with him for almost half an hour. Usually he is obedient and submissive, but this morning he went on and on. He was inconsolable.

Finally, I lost patience and said, "Don't be a bloody cry baby! Suck it up son. Be a man!" and I slammed the phone down.

The sleet hit the windshield and stuck there. It looked like tiny crystal eyes peering in at me. I put on the wipers. Soon snowflakes fluttered down. Heavier and heavier they fell like dead moths, until my windshield wipers stalled. I pulled over onto the shoulder of the road as visibility was almost nil.

"Damn that boy making me late!" I said, growling.

Just then, a shadow emerged through the shield of snow. It was a tall man bending into the wind and swirling snow. He came right up to the driver's door and knocked on the window. I rolled the window down a crack to get a better look at him. "What are you doing?" I asked in annoyance.

"Jest tryin' to get to the next town. I been waitin' for a ride for an hour, but hardly any traffic today. Big blizzard comin', they said on the radio."

"Well then, what in the hell are you doing out in it?" My impatience was growing at an alarming rate. I felt I could strangle somebody.

"Jest tryin, to get to the next town," he repeated calmly.

"You and me both," I muttered. I felt like a fool for having taken my ire out on him. "Here, come around to the passenger side and get in out of the storm," I said in as genially a tone as I could muster.

A gust of freezing air seemed to blow him into the car when he opened the door. He tried to shake the snow from his frayed jacket but had to end up just wiping at it. His old felt hat had two inches of snow piled on top. This he did manage to shake onto the floor.

I had the heater going, and soon there was a film of fog on all the windows from his melting snow. I felt like we were in a sauna.

He sat there with his eyes closed not saying a word, and when I looked over at him, he seemed to feel my gaze. He opened his eyes and looked into mine. The shock of what I saw impelled me to ask, "Sir, are you okay?"

"Yeah, I suppose I am. Jest thawing out I guess."

But there was something heavy in him. His eyes held the look of a man beaten down to the core of emptiness. From the seed shop of pain, he drew each tortured breath, and when I put my hand on his shoulder, he seemed to give way. And there he was, weeping. Great sobs shook his frame.

"What is it? How can I help you?" I asked in alarm.

It was then that I noticed a small burlap sack clutched in his hands. He saw me glancing at the bag.

"It's my boy, you see," he said, as he opened the sack and pulled out an intricately carved wooden container. "It's his urn. I made it myself. I jest have to get to the next town. He was cremated yesterday, and I want to put his ashes in this urn that I made specially for him, not some cardboard box they have him in. His funeral is today. I jest have to get to the next town before it's too late."

His last words, "too late" slammed into me just as the semi-trailer slammed into us.

*Dream *Brandy *Pizzeria
*Devil *Oven *Manager

THE MAKINGS OF A HERO

The pale morning light filtered through the Venetian window shades into the study. Jared awoke with a start. He was still sitting in the old leather recliner where he had dozed off the night before. His first thought was, *Good, thank God, it was only a dream. We are all still here! Hope I haven't overslept again. The twins need to get to school.*

He pulled himself up, and in doing so, knocked over a half-full glass of brandy from the table beside the chair. He didn't seem to notice when his stockinged feet soaked up the mess. He went to the girls' bedroom and saw the rumpled sheets. "Guess they're already up," he muttered.

There was no one in the kitchen. "Oh, my God. I overslept and Meg had to drive the girls to school. I'd better make it up to her or I'll never hear the end of it."

The counters were strewn with dirty plates and crumbs. The table was set with four side plates and glasses. A birthday cake sat crumbling at the far end of the table. In the centre, amidst shrivelled rose petals that had fallen like pink tears, was a crystal vase. Jared took no notice of the mess. He looked at the clock above the stove. It read 11:30 – just time to buy lunch and take it to Meg's office.

Jared was in the car before he realized he was not wearing shoes. "Shit, now I'll be late." He ran back into the study and put on his shoes. The coffee table laden down with empty beer bottles and cigarette butts escaped his notice.

In the pizzeria, Jared called out to Angelo and his wife, "Meg's favourite please and make it hot and quick or I'll be late and catch hell!"

Jared did not observe the look that passed between Angelo and his wife. She just shook her head and whispered, *"Povero diavolo!"*

A patron sitting at a nearby table said quietly, "Poor devil indeed."

Jared grabbed the flat pizza box out of Angelo's hand, said, "Thanks," and without paying ran out the door. Angelo and Maria looked at each other with tear-filled eyes and then went back to the ovens.

The car clock said 12:05 when Jared parked in front of Meg's workplace. "Good, not too late. She'll be surprised."

"Who's that scruff?" the new girl at the reception desk asked her co-worker, Mildred, as Jared approached. Before Mildred could answer, Jared was at the desk.

"Hello Mildred, where's the wife? Got a nice hot pizza for her, right out of the oven."

"Oh Jared, she's not here."

"Damn, am I too late? Did she already go out to lunch? Where? Maybe I can catch her."

"Just a second, Jared. Wait there. I'll be right back." Mildred hurried to the manager's office. "He's here again, Mr. Wilson."

As Mr. Wilson approached Jared, he held out his hand. "Jared, my boy, how are you doing?"

"Fine, fine, I brought Meg some lunch, so I can't talk now. Got to find her. Where did she go?"

Mr. Wilson stammered, "Mm, Jared, Meg hasn't been here for three weeks; you know that now, don't you?"

"What the hell are you saying there, Mr. Big Shot? Where is Meg?" Jared hollered. He threw the pizza across the room and overturned the receptionist's desk. "You better have some answers, mister. He grabbed for the man's shirtfront.

The manager backed away and hissed to Mildred, "Call the police and medics this time."

He tried to placate Jared, but Jared flailed his arms around and kept yelling, "Where is my wife, you bastard?"

It took four policemen and three medics to subdue Jared. He was taken away in a straitjacket, still shouting, Meg! My Meg! My girls!"

The new receptionist looked around at the shambles, "What's going on here?"

No one said a word, but Mildred drew out a newspaper from a drawer and handed it to the girl.

The headlines read: "Mother and twin daughters slain in road rage incident."

*Disaster *Perpetual* Lollygag *Impatient
*Hierarchy *background

CROSSED WIRES

"He may do himself or others harm; he's a disaster waiting to happen," the psychiatrist is saying.

Mario shakes his head and glares at the rotating overhead fan as if to lay the blame above in some airy, other-worldly space.

He says, "The disaster happened twenty-six years ago when my son came into this world; he's had nothing but trouble from day one."

"I know it has been very difficult for you over the years, for both of you, but now, since Marcello is exhibiting more and greater symptoms of schizophrenia, we must consider having him committed. He needs more care than you can give him, Mario. You are exhausted and getting more impatient with his strange behaviours."

"Strange behaviours? It's gone beyond that! Why now he is proclaiming himself a prophet, going around dressed in a white robe and sandals, hasn't shaved for six months, spouting all this nonsense about a great darkening of the skies and other omens of doom.

"His perpetual ranting is killing me. Day and night he raves on and on in remarkable cadence, never missing a beat, always the same words, same inflections, same mantra. If this goes on, I will be the one who will be put away, either for insanity or murder. I love the boy, but I have reached my limit."

Mario's hands are shaking and tears glisten in tired, grief-filled eyes. "He's my son, you know." Mario's voice is plaintive – like the plea of a homeless, starving cat mewing, "Help me or I expire!"

Doctor Rawlins pats Mario's shoulder and says, "It can be arranged for this afternoon. An ambulance will arrive and escort him to the facility. You of course can ride with him."

"Aw, Doctor, does it have to be this way? Can't I just bring him myself?"

"No, Mario. This is best in case he reacts violently. I will of course be at the hospital to meet you both. Now go on home and try to compose yourself. Maybe pack up some of Marcello's belongings if it is feasible for you to do so."

Mario, with shoulders slumped, stumbles to the office door and then turns and shouts in agony, "Oh, my son, I would give anything to have him be just a normal, lollygagging, young man instead of a social enigma and bundle of crossed wires!"

The phone is ringing. Mario pushes himself up from the sofa where he is lying and rushes to answer before the ringing stops. Out of breath, he wheezes, "Hello, Mario here."

There is crackling on the line and then a voice shouts, "Hey Pops! It's Marcello. I'm being released tomorrow morning. Can you pick me up at ten?"

"Are you sure, Marcello? You're sure you feel fine already after only four weeks?"

"Yeah, Pops. Doc says I'm good to go. Just stay on my medication and all will be well."

"Where have I heard that before?" Mario mumbles to himself and then says into the phone, "Good on you, Marcello. Ten it is. See you then, my boy!"

Watching Marcello running towards him, Mario is overcome with joy. "Why, he looks like a teenager again, full of life and hope. Maybe this time is for good," he says aloud.

"Hi Pops. Let's stop for breakfast at the Turnpike. We can sit out on the patio and watch the girls go by."

Mario hugs Marcello close and laughs. "Let's go, my son."

The patio is crowded. People talking, waiters scurrying by, muted laughter, and music thumping in the background.

"Can't make out what you are saying, Marcello," Mario says. "Speak louder, I can't hear above this racket."

"I said, can you hear them singing, Pops?"

"Who, Marcello? All I can hear is a bunch of mumbo jumbo coming from the sound system."

Mario looks at Marcello and sees him looking up at the satiny ice-blue sky, his face a rapture of frightening intensity.

"Oh my God, Marcello, what is happening? What is it?"

Mario looks all about to see if anyone is listening and watching them. No one is paying them any mind.

Suddenly Marcello yells, "Pops, look can you see them? All of them. Angels singing!"

There he is standing, with arms raised, swaying back and forth, shouting halleluiahs.

Before Mario can react, Marcello bolts into the street, laughing, singing full voice. His face is all aglow with a rapturous light. There is a screech of brakes.

As if in slow motion Mario sees his son flung to the pavement. All sound is silenced.

Mario doesn't hear the screams of women, the hurried running of feet, the siren's wail.

He sits, head bowed, and whispers, "Oh Marcello, my son, my son. Where dear God will my boy's place be in the hierarchy of angels? He had better be top gun, for don't you think he deserves it?"

*Auctioneer *Depression *Roses
*Junk *Turtles *Money

ONCE, TWICE, AND GONE

"Going once, going twice. Sold!" The auctioneer's hammer rapped down like a gunshot.

The old man dozing in the back of the crowded room awoke with a cry. But no one paid him any attention. All eyes were riveted on the auctioneer; all ears greedily taking in his words.

"Now folks, the large furniture and heavy objects have been disposed of. Now we will start with the items you have all been waiting for. Yep, all you collectors, pay attention! I know most of you collectors out there are here for this fine collection of Depression glass. Shall we get started? He paused. "Shall we?" he asked again in a teasing voice.

Some patrons yelled, "Yes!" Others muttered, "Just get on with it."

The old man sat up straight and pressed his hands together in anticipation. His face lit up like a sudden lightning flash. He reached into his pocket and felt the twenty-dollar bill his son had given him the day before when he had visited him at the nursing home.

"Here Pop," he had said, "a little spending money. You may want to buy something. I know you like auctions, and I hear Becker's Auction House is holding a sale tomorrow."

Now, the old man leaned forward to listen more closely to the bidding. But ... all the bidding started at fifty dollars.

The auctioneer held up piece after piece of the Depression glass, extolling the beauty of the items. "And here we have the Peacock and Wild Rose, nine-inch, footed bowl, the Little Jewel Diamond Block bowl, the Florentine creamer, the Cone Design green sherbet set." On and on the auctioneer droned.

Piece after piece was claimed, and the old man shrunk deeper and deeper into himself. He couldn't even bid.

Thirty minutes later and the Depression glass was all sold, even the drinking glasses. People filed out and soon the place was empty. The old man shuffled up to the front of the room. There were only empty boxes where the Depression glass had been stored. He pushed his hands into the straw packing, searching, hoping there was one piece left.

Something hard, sharp! He jerked his hand out of the box. A finger was bleeding slightly. He licked the blood off. Gingerly, this time, he searched until he found the object. Tenderly, he pulled a pink-coloured glass from the straw. The rim was chipped.

He held the glass up to the light, and there she was, his beloved wife. The translucent blush of youth gave her face a liveliness, a smooth iridescence...

The gentle wind of remembrance settled upon the old man, and he sighed the length of the years.

She was smiling, holding up a rose-coloured drinking glass that she had just removed from the Quaker Oat box. "Oh, isn't it beautiful, Alex? And all for free! We are going to eat a lot of oats, my darling." She laughed. "I want the whole set."

"And you shall have them," he had said while smothering her face with kisses and secretly wishing he could buy her the real crystal she deserved, not that machine-made stuff.

He was jolted out of his reverie when a young worker said, "Hey, mister, time to go. We want to close now."

Alex jolted back into real time. He said, "Here is twenty dollars for this glass."

The young man examined the glass and said, "Hey, it's a piece of junk. Keep it, old man. Now, please get out of here."

Alex walked out of the auction house clutching the chipped glass. On the street he held it up to the sunlight. A rosy glow filtered through the glass. Alex smiled.

He walked on, stopping at the corner store where flowers were displayed in colourful rows outside. He found the roses. "Yellow, your favourite, my darling. One for you, one for me."

He entered the store, walked to the candy display and picked up a big box of Turtles. "That will be twelve dollars for the Turtles and five dollars for the roses,"

He gave the clerk the twenty-dollar bill.

Alex pocketed the change, put the two yellow roses into the chipped Depression glass, popped a turtle into his mouth, and shuffled back towards his home.

"If I hurry, I can catch the five o'clock news," he said aloud to no one in particular.

*Transference *Tree house *Oshmygosh
*Mountains *Octaves *Obnoxious

MY HUSBAND

Demi sat with her mother, Gladys, at the secluded table in Jim's Bar. A tight twosome, straining to breaking point in their efforts to be civil to each other.

"Oshmygosh! Your husband can't be thinking of taking a year off, leaving this thriving business, and taking you and the kids to Italy just on a silly whim!" Gladys chirped. She gave a tight little smile that did not quite show teeth.

"Why must you always refer to Jim as 'my husband', Mother? We've been married for fifteen years, and you have never called him 'Jim'. It's either 'your husband' or 'him' or 'he' or 'that man you are married to'. I'm tired of it, Mother! His name is Jim. You are so … so … irritating!" Demi wanted to say "obnoxious" but did not quite have the stamina to withstand the rebuttal that would blast back at her.

"Oshmygosh! There you go again, Demi, making mountains out of mole-hills. I'm just asking why he is going to give up your lovely situation to go to Italy, of all places. Where is this Italian town Antrodoco, anyway? On the toe of Italy I suppose, not in Tuscany, where it is sunny and warm. He must be off his rocker."

Demi held the edges of the table tightly, pressed her lips together tightly, screwed her control mechanism tightly within herself, and rigidly

167

replied, "Of all people I know, he is the sanest. I support him all the way, Mother, so please let's just change the subject. We are going, and that is the end of it. And ... for your information, Antrodoco is not on the toe of Italy. It is in central Italy!"

"Oshmygosh! What will become of me? Have you thought of that? No, I am sure you haven't. Selfish, you and that man you are married to! Who will I have my afternoon nip with? Who is going to run this bar while you and your husband are away gallivanting in Italy of all places? Taking my grandchildren from me is pure elder abuse!" Gladys' voice had risen a few octaves, and other customers were moving further away from their table.

"We need a break, Mother, and a year off is nothing compared to the time we have spent running this place and ... and ..."

"Say it, Demi! And ... putting up with your obnoxious mother!" Her voice was a squall.

Suddenly Demi was laughing. Great sobs of air spurted out of her in joyous abandonment. "There is such a thing as transference of thought mother! Isn't it wonderful? You finally admit that you are obnoxious."

Still shaking with giggles and wiping away tears with a paper serviette, Demi stood and patted her mother's head tentatively as if patting a vicious cat that might at any moment scratch her eyes out.

"Goodbye, Mother. We are off tonight."

Gladys howled, "Oshmygosh! That husband of yours will have you all living in a tree house in that godforsaken Antrodoco. What's there? Only mountains and ignorant peasants. Yes, ignorant, ignorant!"

Demi left her mother screaming profanities and thought to herself, *Shove it, Mom, right up your 'oshmygosh'.*

The sun was slipping down the back of the mountain, leaving its fulvous light behind.

Jim's face looks like a warrior's, chiselled in precious gold. My warrior, all mine, Demi thought as she laid her head on Jim's shoulder and sighed. "I will be sorry to leave Antrodoco, Jim. It has been a wonderful year, hasn't it, my husband?"

As the words "my husband" echoed in her head, she shivered remembering her mother.

"Ah, Demi," Jim began. "I've been thinking. How about we stay on here indefinitely?"

"Are you serious?"

"Yep."

"What would we do? How would we survive without work? Where would the kids go to school?"

"The kids adore it here. They have picked up the language in just a year. The people love us. I've been scouting around, and I've found a nice, little spot where we can open a small bar and grill. We have enough to get started. What do you say, Demi?"

"My husband, the entrepreneur." Demi smiled. "Yes, yes, yes!"

The phone call to Gladys went rather well, Demi was later to say, as she recounted it to Jim.

"No Mother, we are not returning, and we now live in a lovely cottage on a hill overlooking the town. No, not a treehouse. My husband? You mean Jim, don't you? Oh, he is wonderful. He is a beacon of light, sturdy and strong as a lighthouse. The people love him.

"We are opening a small bar. No, not the same name 'Jim's Bar', as in Canada. Now it is a name I thought very appropriate. It is called 'Mia Marito Bar and Grill'. No, not so foreign a name, for you at least, Mother. It means, 'My Husband's Bar and Grill'!"

*Amble *Scintillating *Entitlement
*Helipad *Elevator

BIGMOUTH CANYON

The water below the cliffs of the Bigmouth Canyon seems to amble along at a slow, leisurely pace, but those who know the Bunco River are well acquainted with its treachery. It lives up to its name. It is a trickster with deep undercurrents and whirlpools that can swallow a man ... or a woman, for that matter. The Bunco never burps up or regurgitates its victims.

And ... this was all Dr. Clifford needed to know; the months of tedious research was now complete. He could get on with it. She was becoming a threat to his marriage.

"No fuss, no muss, no bother," he hummed, as he tapped out the invitation, his fingers dancing lightly on the keyboard.

Five minutes later, a reply. "Alone at last. Where's wifey off to this time? I would be delighted to have lunch with you tomorrow. Same time, same place, Cliffy darling."

A heart-pounding scintillating moment and rush of adrenaline almost knocked him off his feet as he read her response. As he jumped up, he tripped on the untied laces of his right foot running shoe. "Damn! I thought I tied my laces."

The taxi dropped her off at the estate at noon. "What is this place?" the cabbie asked. "It looks like a mansion, and look, there is even a helipad over in that field."

"It's a so-called rest home for the wealthy, like a hospital, really, for all those old fogeys with lots of dough."

"Well, what are you doing here then?"

"I work here sometimes."

"Yeah, I bet you do," the driver mumbled as he counted out her change.

"*No tip, cheap bag*," he thought as he watched her totter off on heels as high and slim as chop sticks. "Glad I got a real woman at home waitin' for me." He crossed himself and kissed the Saint Theresa doll bobbing on the dashboard.

The private entrance to Dr. Clifford's residence on the top floor of the Manor House Rest Home was situated at the side of the building. She pressed the button in the oak-lined elevator and was whisked up to the fifth floor. The door opened directly into the wide, richly ornamented foyer, where Dr. Clifford stood waiting.

As he bent to kiss her, he stumbled and almost knocked her over. "Damn, I forgot to lace up my shoe again."

"Why do you wear those running shoes, anyhow? Even in a suit you wear them," she said.

I wear what I like, when I like," he snapped in a voice of entitlement. "Lunch is set out in the living room today. Come along." He grabbed her around the waist and pushed her in front of him.

"Don't get feisty yet. Let's eat first."

"Of course, my dear. Of course," he said aloud but finished his sentence silently, "*even criminals are allowed a last meal*."

She droned on and on throughout the luncheon. Finally, he poured the final glass of wine. She was already fumbling, trying to raise the glass to her drooping lips.

He carried her to the bedroom. She laughed, "I think I'm high. Oh my gosh, what's that wheelchair doing by the bed?"

She giggled as he strapped her in. "Is this a new game, Cliffy?" she slurred and then dropped her head.

It was 2:00 a.m. when he wheeled her, wrapped tightly in a blanket, to the helicopter. "An emergency. I'm flying tonight," he told the night watchman on duty, who knew it was nothing out of the ordinary with the old ones.

He opened the passenger door, carried her from the wheelchair and kicked the wheelchair away.

It only took twenty minutes to reach the canyon. There was only a full moon to witness the arbitrary transaction as the unfortunate paramour plunged into the Bunco from the hovering helicopter.

"Wish I could have seen the landing in the daylight," the doctor chortled. "Next one for sure. This is the best one yet. Better get back now."

He booked a Bigmouth Canyon tour for his wife and himself the following month.

"Please, people," the young sweet-faced tour guide said, "Don't step too close to the edge of the cliff. It's a long way down."

Everyone gingerly moved away except Dr. Clifford. His wife tried to draw him back, but he pulled himself from her grasp. "I just want to get a better look." As he moved closer to the rim, his foot caught on one of his untied running shoe laces. He stumbled and tried to balance himself.

His wife watched in horror, as arms flailing like helicopter blades, Cliffy nosedived down, down, into the Bunco ... where it is said that a man, or even a woman, will never be regurgitated.

A silent vigil was held a few weeks later, on a sunny afternoon, at the Manor Rest Home.

An eagle silently flew high over the Bigmouth Canyon that same sunny afternoon, and the Bunco River slyly meandered along, hiding her secrets beneath her smooth blue skirts.

*Frog *Cow *Elephant *Foreign
*Filament *Innate *Farrago

A FARRAGO OF FACT
AND MYTH

It was the day of the full moon when all the inhabitants of the protected animal reserve in India got together for the annual Harvest Moon Shindig. On this day, a foreign element had been injected into the yearly gathering. Two strangers from Canada had arrived at the reserve: a beaver, wounded by a woodsman's cleaver, and a Canada goose with a wing in a sling.

Almost immediately, the beaver began to gnaw at the only tree near the stream that emptied into a lake. It then jumped into the water and slapped its tail, making a great racket! The Canada goose got all excited and began to call out, sounding like a braying fishwife and a vehicle horn at full volume. Both animals were nervous and confused by the exotic smells and new hot surroundings.

It was the frog that croaked out and calmed them down. He welcomed them to the reserve and told them about the party that was about to begin. "You will be our honoured guests," he said in his deep hoarse voice. "You are welcome here."

Not everyone felt that way. The cows in the group started to mumble that they were the ones that deserved the greatest honour. "Are we not the sacred cows of India? Did Gandhi not say he 'would never kill a cow for a human or a human for a cow'? We are the symbol of India!" They began to dance and moo loudly in their boastful, lowing way, which seemed to irritate all the other animals.

The mishmash really got started when Regena, a retired circus elephant, boasted about her innate, total recall ability. She was usually circumspect and careful not to reveal all the tidbits of gossip and other private matters pertaining to her friends that she had heard over the years, but this display of superiority annoyed her greatly.

Their behaviour loosened her tongue, so to speak. "Do you cows forget why you are here? Well I sure don't. Wasn't it you, fancy talking Reza, that walked right into traffic and lay there with a broken hip until one of the keepers dragged you here on a cart tied behind his bicycle? You weren't singing your happy tune then, were you? And you Miss Uppity Udders … You were dressed in some kind of red robe and golden scarf that had choked you, when they brought you here, and what did you say that night? Regena mimicked, 'Oh, thank you, dear animals, you are so kind to take me in and make me feel welcome.'"

The cows stopped dancing and lowing, their wide eyes wider and sadder than the animals had ever seen before.

"Wow!" said the Canada goose, "you sure got a memory there, lady, but you ain't got nothing on me."

"Ha! That's where you are wrong Mr. Goosey," Regena said condescendingly. "Wasn't it you, on your trip over the Hudson River that day, that brought the plane down? You still haven't fully recovered, have you? I know they found your feather in Engine #1."

The Canada goose pulled his brown body up and bowed his black head and neck, his white cheeks now blushing and the white of his chinstrap trembling. A tear rolled down his beak, and he meekly said, "Yeah, that was me and my brother. He didn't make it."

What's this turning into? The frog thought. Then he piped up, or rather, croaked, "Now, don't you get so self-righteous, Regena dear. Didn't they brainwash you at the circus by tying your leg with a rope so you wouldn't run away? Aren't you still tied by a single filament to your post? You can't even break that fragile tie to the past. So who are you to judge my dear?"

All was silent. It felt like a wake until the wounded loon floating on the small lake began to laugh at the moon that had risen over the horizon. A hyena also laughed and a grey wolf howled.

Smiles appeared here and there in the crowd, and suddenly, the crane whooped, the frog croaked, the elephant trumpeted, the cows mooed, the beaver clapped, the goose sang "O Canada" in a piercing falsetto, and the townspeople living near the reserve plugged their ears, groaned, and tried to go back to sleep.

*Embody *Pucker *Buttercup
*Demonstration *Canvas

THE EMBODIMENT
OF CAPITALISM

Eugenia was titillated; excitement poured out of her. At last, she could do something great for the cause. She had waited long enough to make the supreme sacrifice. As she clutched the buttercup-yellow canvas bag to her chest she imagined she could hear time ticking, keeping up with her racing heartbeat.

The demonstration against poverty was set for 5:00 p.m., during rush hour when the foot and vehicle traffic were at a peak. All she had to do was to make her way into the middle of the crowd, take a deep breath, and open the bag. This would set off the mechanism, and it would all be over. She knew she would be on the way to her Elysium but she would die a hero.

A man stood nearby surreptitiously watching Eugenia.

High above the metropolis, on the other side of the city, two men sat smiling. They were smoking cigars, sipping brandy, and watching the demonstration on a giant TV screen.

"Do you think she will do it? Two million says she won't."

"I'm not entirely sure, but if she opens the bag, we will know she could be one of us. I'll anti it up to three million. I'm pretty sure of her."

"You're on. Three million says she won't open the bag."

"Look at that crowd. Poor suckers, thinking that any demonstration will ever change anything."

"Let them dream. Let them dream. Puppets, they are only puppets."

"Yes, only we need them. Without the sheeple we have no dominion."

"Truer words were never spoken, my friend."

Their smiles grew broader.

Eugenia pushed her way further into the crowd. She elbowed her way past a tall man with a child on his shoulders. As she did so, she stepped on a little boy's foot.

"Ouch, Daddy, that lady stepped on my foot," he cried out.

"Never mind, son. I'm sure she didn't mean no harm."

Eugenia bent down to apologize, hoping not to draw attention to herself, but she made the mistake of looking into the child's eyes. The eyes were green with little sparkles of brown light, so pure and innocent.

Just then the little girl perched on the father's shoulder bent down and touched Eugenia's head. "Daddy, this lady looks like mommy. She has the same colour hair, all gold, just like mommy."

A convulsion of emotions quaked through Eugenia. Tears cascaded down her cheeks. *What am I doing? Who have I turned into? Oh, my God!*

Eugenia clutched the canvas bag and pushed her way out of the crowd. When free, she ran to the city park. She threw the bag into a garbage receptacle. Panting and moaning, she made her way to the subway.

What will I tell them? What will they do to me? she thought. Another part of her said aloud, "I don't care!"

Eugenia was escorted into the stateroom by a burly, well-dressed attendant. She wrung her hands then tried to smooth the pucker in her skirt as she stood, head bowed, in front of the two men.

They remained seated, talking in low voices, and did not acknowledge her presence.

Minutes passed. Eugenia could stand it no longer. She shouted, "I couldn't do it! I just couldn't. You see there was this …"

The two men held up their hands to silence her. One of them motioned to the attendant who opened the door. A svelte woman came through holding the buttercup-yellow canvas bag.

"Give it to her," both men ordered.

Eugenia paled as her shaking hands clutched the bag.

"Open it!" both men demanded.

Slowly Eugenia pulled on the straps. The bag opened. Nothing happened! Eugenia fell to the floor.

"Get up, you stupid cow! Empty the bag."

Eugenia turned the bag upside down and out fluttered hundreds of bills, a sealed envelope, and a large ticking clock.

The two men laughed uproariously.

"I ... I don't understand," Eugenia stammered.

"Count them, then open the envelope and read what it says."

Kneeling, Eugenia began counting the bills. Finally, she murmured, "One million dollars."

Opening the envelope, she read, "You have proven yourself. Your loyalty has earned you a million dollars and a trusted place in the world order."

"What of the cause of disruption?" Eugenia asked.

"Shall we explain?" one man said to the other.

"Yes. You see, Eugenia, we thought we saw something in you called loyalty, but what a disappointment you are. Your ignorant view of a cause meant nothing to us. We imagined you could pass our test, but how wrong I was! If you had fulfilled your commitment, you could have been one of us. We need strong bricks to build our empire."

He shook his head and growled, "Get her out of my sight!"

The other man howled with laughter. "I win. How about my three million?"

Positive *Sentimental* *Customs Officer*
Candour *Alarm* *Dolt*

A POSITIVE OUTCOME

The old Chevy Coupe is idling at the border crossing. The mellow strains of Nat King Cole singing, "I love you for sentimental reasons," wafts out of the open window as the elderly man and woman sing along.

This is the fifty-fifth anniversary of their marriage, and they are on their way to Seattle to recapture the excitement of those heady days.

A customs officer sticks his head through the window and yells, "Hey Pops, turn off that bloody racket and cut your engine. You should know better than that."

Maggie reaches over and turns the knob of the radio. Jackson switches off the engine. In the brief silence that follows Maggie leans over her husband and smiles at the officer before berating him.

"Officer, you need not take on that impolite tone with us. We are just on our second honeymoon, for heaven's sake! Where are your manners? Weren't you taught to respect your elders?"

Her candour throws the officer. He reddens and growls, "Exit the car, both of you!"

Jackson tightens his grip on the steering wheel and says, "You are not acting in a responsible manner, young man. We have to make it to Seattle by 3:00 p.m. or our reservation will be cancelled. Have a heart."

"Exit the car!" the officer repeats. His voice is rising, and he is becoming flustered. "You will be removed if you do not comply!"

The couple remain seated. They stare straight ahead, jaws set tight.

The officer speaks into his radio and soon two other officers arrive at the scene. One is burly, the other slim and stern.

The burly man repeats, "Exit the car, both of you, or you will be removed!"

"We are just on our way to Seattle to celebrate our fifty-fifth anniversary," Maggie calls out.

"Why do we have to get out of the car?" Jackson still grips the steering wheel. His knuckles are white. "We haven't done anything to warrant this kind of treatment!"

"Okay, time to show who's boss," the slim officer says to the others. He reaches for the door handle, but Maggie has leaned over and locked the driver's door. She then locks her door. Jackson quickly rolls up his window.

The officers are cursing under their breaths and shaking their heads. "What the hell are we going to do about this situation?" the burly officer asks.

Cars are backed up behind the Chevy, and people are getting out of their cars to see what the holdup is.

The slim officer draws his gun and taps it on the driver's window. Jackson takes his hands off the steering wheel and rolls down his window. "All we want is to get to Seattle before 3:00 p.m. What's the big problem? Why do we have to get out of the car? Can't you see we are no threat to you?"

All three officers yell, "Exit the car immediately!" Their guns are drawn.

"Okay, okay." Jackson opens his door and steps onto the pavement. He tries to walk around the car to Maggie's door but is stopped by the officers.

"Exit the car!" they yell at Maggie. She opens her door but does not step out.

"You don't understand," Jackson tries to say, but he is pushed aside as the burly officer goes around to the passenger door.

He reaches into the car and pulls on Maggie's arm. "Get out, woman, or you are in real trouble!" He yanks her out of her seat, and she falls to the pavement. "Get up, stand up!" he orders.

"Maggie's voice cuts through the crowd as she screams, "I can't, you dolt. I only have one leg!"

The onlookers have been voicing their discontent, but upon seeing this treatment of a disabled woman, they burst into loud exclamations of disgust and alarm.

"We're going to have a riot on our hands if we don't get this under control," the officers declare to each other. They help Maggie up and settle her back into the car. "Okay folks, show's over. Back to your vehicles!"

Jackson is standing with his head in his hands.

"You can leave, but in the future do not think you can argue with a customs officer and tell him to watch his manners, understood?" the first officer says. "This could have been a far from positive outcome for you, my friend. I hope you have learned from it."

"Oh, yes sir!" Jackson says, and to show no hard feelings, he shakes the officer's hand. As they drive through the gate, Maggie waves happily to the officers.

That evening as Maggie and Jackson toast each other on the occasion of their fifty-fifth wedding anniversary, they laugh, roll on the bed, and fling hundreds of tight little packets of cocaine high into the air.

Jackson says, "Talk about a positive outcome. It works, one of many. We'll have enough money to finance our future!"

"We'll only do this for sentimental reasons," Maggie jibes.

They squeal in delight.

*Anguish *Pterodactyl* Effigy
*Heartthrob *Ancestral *Snowball

AN APOLOGY
DOESN'T CUT IT

Two things happened that day, well maybe three, no five. Actually, it may have been six, I forget. It was a long time ago, seventy years to be exact. I was twelve.

Norman, my secret heartthrob, threw a snowball at me in the schoolyard. That's … Count One.

I threw one back, and it hit him right in the face. That's … Count Two.

Miss English, the upright, uptight Catholic principal saw what I did and because throwing snowballs was forbidden, she called me into her classroom, before the bell rang, of course, so we were alone.

She hauled out the leather strap and said, "Hold out your hands, you naughty girl!"

One – two – three – four – five – on each hand. I think she got off on inflicting pain, looking to see if I would cry. Of course I didn't. I never cried back then. This was nothing compared to Pappa's razor belt. I was no sissy. My anguish came later. This was Count … Three.

Count Four … came when I walked up the stairs to my grade six classroom with all the kids staring at me, some laughing, others with eyes down in sympathy.

Count Five ... When thoughts and feelings thundered and cascaded into my mind like a lightning storm. Shame, anger, guilt, confusion, sadness, mostly sadness, as I realized that Norman, who I thought was my knight, was a bloody coward for not coming forward and saying he had lobbed the first snowball at me. So much for a British guy.

Count Six ... Ancestral Revenge. Nobody screws with the Italian Mob!

Miss Paterson, my art teacher, knew what had happened. She patted my shoulder and then said, "Julia, you are a good girl and a great artist. Your drawing is exceptional."

Then my plan was born. For weeks I worked on it in the basement of Pappa's home. I never called this place mine. I constructed a giant pterodactyl, the huge prehistoric, flying lizard with the long, long neck just like Miss English's. I used coat hangers for the bones and covered them with paper mache, using old newspapers, water, and flour that I stole from Gramma's pantry.

It took two weeks, but those were excruciating days of payback magic. Finally, my creation was ready. That night at midnight, I crept down to the basement from my attic bedroom, careful not to awaken my three sisters. I wrapped a rope around my arm and hauled that huge monstrosity outside and carried it to the schoolyard.

The next morning, Gramma didn't have to yell at me to get up. I was quiet when she pulled my hair into braids. I gobbled down the oatmeal and ran out the door as she slapped me and bawled out her usual farewell, *"Va via!"*

Yeah, okay, Gramma, I'll go away fast, I thought to myself.

I was early. No one was in the schoolyard yet ...

I sat on the steps and watched as a few kids arrived and then more and more. Soon they were all shouting and laughing and pointing at the basketball hoop, where hung by the long, scrawny neck, the effigy of Miss English.

Miss English finally came out to see what the ruckus was all about. She hollered for the janitor to pull down the abomination, as she called it.

I heard Miss Paterson and the janitor exchanging words at lunchtime. They would often hold hands secretly in his cubbyhole of an office. As I passed the door, I heard the janitor laughingly say, "The face on that old flying dinosaur sure did look familiar! Wonder who did that?"

I heard no answer from Miss Patterson.

The next year on Valentine's Day, when I was in grade eight, there was a knock on the classroom door. The teacher spoke to someone and then closed the door. He turned around and in his arms was a big bouquet of flowers, a box of chocolates, and a pink card.

"For you, madam," the teacher said, as he bowed and handed the gifts to me.

I must have turned red because my face was burning. Everyone was staring. The card said: "I'm a jerk and a big coward. Sorry. Norman."

*Secrets *Moon *Creation
*Mother *Firefly *Ice

TALKING TO THE WIND

I talk to the Wind.

Often at night, when the wolves of sadness and grief howl and there seems no redress for the wild antics of the world, I ask the Wind for its help in understanding the "why".

On other nights, the Wind will whisper secrets to me. This is when I know that there will always be good in the world.

When the moon is full and the Wind tickles the trees and makes the leaves jiggle in laughter, it tells me stories, like the one I will relate to you now. It is called:

TEARS OF MOTHER EARTH
Drop by silent drop
Filling oceans of the world
Tears of Mother Earth

There is a place where days slip into the past and tomorrows are born, where Nature balances the seasons and all things on the scales of time, where the Wind whispers its secrets to Mother Earth. It is here, in this sacred place that the Wind found her crying.

"Why do you cry Great Mother?" asked the Wind in consternation.

"Oh, Mighty Wind, my emissary, I cannot sleep; I cannot rest with all the commotion upon my breast. I greatly fear for all creation." She groaned in her sorrow.

"Now, now," soothed the Wind. "You must think of happier times. Do you not remember happier times, Great Mother?"

"Happier times? ... Ah, yes, I remember ..." She sighed mournfully. "I remember laughing for sheer joy with the loon on a lake in the moonlight, while fireflies blinked on and off in the forest.

"And ... in those forests, those mystic forests that grew up creatures and gave them homes were trees that reached up to the sun in the summer and bent low in the winter, laden with snow. I too was covered by the snow and wrapped in its soft, white blanket until spring came, singing its soft, enchanting song. This is when I gathered rocks and sand in my great apron at the base of the glacier, as tiny rivulets of water flowed from within that mountain of ice.

"I tasted sweet rain as it fell, clean and pure, filling up my rivers and rushing down my waterfalls.

"On a summer's day I smelled the heady scent of roses and watched the bees seek out their silky, hidden centres. I saw big, black butterflies kissing red geraniums in the sunshine.

"I heard the cry of gulls in loud competition with crashing waves, along a rocky shore, while overhead the eagle soared higher and higher to embrace the golden dawn.

"I thrilled to feel the great spirit of the buffalo as they thundered across my plains.

"But now ...

"Soon to be gone. All gone. Even my cicadas are becoming silent."

"Great Mother, not so, hear what I have to say," murmured the Wind.

"Today as I travelled among the trees, setting the leaves in motion, I saw a little naked bird fall from its nest and crash itself upon the pavement below."

"Oh! More grief!" cried out the Great Mother.

"Not so, not so," went on the Wind.

He continued. "Many people went by; 'disgusting, dirty', they said. Even a cat was disdainful, but then a small boy happened along. As he saw the tiny, featherless mass, he cried out, and on his knees, took a closer look. 'Poor little bird,' he said with tears in his eyes. He wrapped the bird in his handkerchief, and as he buried it deep under the willow tree, he said a little prayer. Then he walked slowly home.

"Great Mother, this is the story I report today. There is hope, for I saw the future in that child's eyes."

Mother Earth pondered on what she had heard and finally said hopefully, "Perhaps all is not lost, for did you not say you saw the future in that child's eyes?"

"Yes, yes," rustled the Wind as he kissed the Great Mother goodbye and wafted its way over the great divide, where the sky caresses the sea.

"Still …" sighed the Wind as it glided on its way …

"All is not well, when mothers weep alone."

*Fiddle *Cathedral *Zoo
*Miracle *Pudding *Dust

THE CONFESSIONAL

The sky above Calgary is high and blue today. I sit on the bank of the Elbow River and watch the shallow current slide like silk over rock outcroppings near the shore. But further out, the current can change like Pa does most nights into a raging demon that can suck you under and make you fight for your life.

I hear Ma's voice in my head, "You're my good boy, Rusty."

It's the first day of summer holidays, and I should be helping Ma deliver the ironing, but I just had to get away to think. And I am thinking, about Pa mostly. He wasn't always this way Ma tells me, but I can't remember him singing the songs of Ireland, nor have I heard him play the fiddle. I have never seen the ancient bodhran drum that Ma says he brought with him to Canada. These thoughts niggle in my mind, almost drilling a hole.

I had better be on my way home. It's after five. Ma will be upset.

I walk the path by the Sacred Heart Convent toward the cathedral. As I walk, I think of Ma's words. "Your pa has beautiful handwriting. He was taught in Ireland and England before coming to Canada." I remember her pursed lips, "It is too bad that his character no longer matches the sweeping ebb and flow of the graceful script."

I am thinking that the only things that ebb and flow around Pa are his foul moods and the whisky. I am almost at the cathedral. As I look up, I am surprised to see Pa climbing the cathedral steps and pushing open the heavy oak doors. I can't believe my eyes. Curiosity makes me follow him inside, being careful he does not see me. There he is blessing himself with the holy water, his hands making the sign of the cross and little drops of holy water running down his face like tears. He shuffles his way over to the confessional, sidles in, and pulls the grey window curtain shut behind him.

I am astounded. This is the man that says, "The confessional looks like the outhouse and a visit to the one can't compare in satisfaction to the other. In function," he clarifies.

I'm afraid the stained-glass windows will crack and the pews will run out of the church in alarm. But no, the candles at the altar stand don't even flicker, the stoic faces of the statues of the saints do not change expression, and the incense censer doesn't explode in a sulphuric blast. The old women dressed in black still mutter their mantras at the stations of the cross, genuflecting and bowing like possessed crows. No smoke blows out of the confessional where Pa is probably bullshitting his way out of something.

I know I had better blow on out of this quiet place of worship before Pa comes out and sees that I may have witnessed a real live miracle.

I run the six blocks home as if the devil himself is chasing me.

When I clatter through the kitchen door, my ma says in a voice on the verge of a scream, "Rusty, you're late again, now your supper's cold."

I know why Ma sounds this way; she's afraid I'm turning into Pa. What she doesn't know is that of all the people in the world, my pa is the last one that I would want to be like. I have his red hair and that's enough for me.

She ladles out the soup, lukewarm now, and says, "Wash your hands and then sit down and eat." I am spooning the last of the soup into my mouth when Pa walks through the door.

My two little sisters who have been chatting over their pudding seem to get smaller as they hunch their shoulders into themselves. Ma looks startled. He's never here for supper, but here he is and he's sober.

Pa gives out a big whoop and kisses Ma right on the lips, and then he pulls out a bunch of flowers from behind his back. As she takes them, I see her face flush like a sunset, all rosy and bright.

"Oh Jack, they're lovely," she croons. But then I see her eyes harden a little, "What's the occasion, Jack?"

"Does there have to be an occasion for a man to honour his wife?" he glibly replies.

Then heaven rattles in disbelief. I almost fall off my chair. My two sisters gape, mouths wide open, pudding dripping down their chins. Pa picks Ma up and swings her around like Fred Astaire swings Ginger Rogers in the movies! Both of them are laughing and shrieking like banshees, Pa's low voice and Ma's giddy soprano blending into a cacophony of joyous sound.

All I can think is, what is he up to?

The next morning he is not up at all. He lies there white as plaster and the dry heaves almost cough up his guts. Ma is worried and sends me off to the Kwality Chick Hatchery, where Pa works. I have a note for the manager. Ma says that we are so lucky that Pa has a job during these days of hardship when others on the prairies are eating only dust. Ma also says that we are living poorer than poor because of Pa's goings-on and love of the drink.

Pa keeps the books at the hatchery, and just before Easter he helps put dye in the egg embryos so that when the chicks hatch, they are coloured all shades. The chicks are a fluffy pink, bright yellow, mauve, and blue. They are displayed in the front window for the kids. All I know is that I'm sick of running the nine blocks to the hatchery to make more excuses for my pa. I do it every morning for three more days and then I get a new order from Ma.

"Run for the priest, Pa is dying!"

As I run, I wonder if this has anything to do with Pa's confession the other day. Is he going to Glory or to Hell for his penance?

I get back home before the priest arrives. Before I enter the house, I hear Pa screaming. I run to the bedroom, and there he is wound up in the sheets, squirming, sweating, eyes wild and staring. He is brushing at himself, hollering, "Get them off. Get them off."

I don't see anything, and Ma is trying to hold him down. Then he sees something else we don't. He screeches worse than a rabbit when it is grabbed by a hawk. He yells that the roses on the wallpaper are bleeding rivers of blood and drowning him. Now he is gasping and snorting like Aunt Louisa's pet potbellied pig.

"Mama," I shout over the ruckus. "I'm going to call the ambulance." But she doesn't hear. She is standing over Pa, bawling like a baby, wringing her hands as if they are wet dishrags.

I am out of breath when I get to the corner store where they have a phone. "Call the ambulance. Pa is dying!" I gasp and sputter until old Mr. Camelli understands. He picks up the phone and asks the operator for the ambulance.

When I get home, I feel like the rag picker's poor old nag. I am sweating and panting. The priest, Father O'Connor, is patting my ma, muttering his stock phrases of comfort into her ear. He sees me and rumples my damp hair and then quickly recoils and wipes the sweat off his hand onto his hanky that he draws out from some hidden place in his cassock.

"Good boy, Rusty. Your dad needs a doctor more than a priest right now." He says this because he can't get near my pa, what with the thrashing and yelling.

The ambulance finally arrives and the attendants tie Pa up in some kind of white jacket. He is hauled away with sirens blasting. The neighbours stand gawking, pointing, and talking in whispers.

Three weeks pass. Pa is still in the hospital. Ma begs for Relief so we get a chit from the government. Every night, we kneel as a family and pray for Pa. My little sisters' lisping voices pleading for God to bring Pa home kind of irritate me. I'm thinking of how quiet it has been around here; no curses echoing off the walls, no stink of puke and stale whisky-breath blowing in my face when I stand between Pa and Ma, no fear-stilled faces of my sisters, no black bruises hiding behind Mama's rouge and powder. Why, I wonder, would God want to bring this back into our lives, but I go along with the ritual just to calm Ma.

It is Thursday and my sisters and I have our mouths full of cookie pieces as we walk home from the Dad's Cookie Company that gives free broken cookies to kids once a week during the summer. I carry a brown paper bag with some for Ma.

When we reach home, we see neighbours all lined up at the door. We squeeze past and see Ma all smiles and wearing her best dress standing behind Pa, who is sitting on a kitchen chair as if he were "King of the Castle". People are shaking his hand and saying how good he looks and "Welcome home, Jack". I can't believe this is Pa. His face is not all puffy and red. His shoulders are straight and strong like a soldier's. His voice is clear, his brogue lilting and mellow and sounding like soft thunder.

All at once, I don't know why, but tears are running down my face like Niagara Falls. I am blubbering like a baby. Pa jumps up and puts me in a hug that squeezes the sobs out of me even more. He smells of Old Spice and fresh plums. I drink him in and melt into his body. I never, ever felt so close to anyone, so part of someone, so loved. He picks me up, all twelve years of me, and sits me on his lap. I don't care. I don't think. I only know that Pa is home, not in Glory or in Hell. With my head on his shoulder, I close my eyes.

When I open them, the neighbours, Ma, and my sisters are all gone. Only the faint caw of a crow and the rustle of the window curtain break the stillness.

Pa gets his old job back at the chick hatchery. Ma still takes in ironing. My sisters still play with their dollies. I still cannot believe the change in Pa, and I am getting more and more jittery as the weeks pass by, wondering if it will last. I am also feeling guilty that I spied on Pa that day when he went into the confessional. I feel like Judas because I didn't really pray for Pa to come home.

It is Labour Day. School starts this week. We are on the big, green lawn at the zoo on St. George's Island. Pa has his head in Ma's lap, and she is stroking his hair, murmuring something to him. His eyes are closed. A small, contented smile is tickling his face. My sisters are playing near the swings. I am sitting on the grass with my arms around my knees, looking at Ma and Pa, lying there so peaceful and happy.

But … I know this is the day that I have to tell Pa of my betrayal.

He looks up and sees me looking at them. It is almost as if he knows what I am thinking for he gently pushes Ma's hands away and gets up.

"Rusty, let's go for a little walk."

I can't look Pa in the eye. I walk over to a bench under a tree and Pa joins me. Pa asks, "What is bothering you boy?"

I stammer out my confession. I tell him how I spied on him at the cathedral, how I hated him and didn't want him to come home, how I worry that he will start drinking again. After I say these words, my head feels like it's singing "Ave Maria".

To my surprise, Pa puts his arm around me. He says, "I have something to tell you too." He takes a deep breath.

"The day you saw me go into the confessional was the day my life changed forever. I was walking down Seventeenth Avenue after work, thinking about getting some whisky, when I happened to glance over the street. Right there across from me was this dog, an Irish setter, all sparkling and a bronzy red. Its coat was shining, its eyes too, when they caught my eye. I knew right then that the dog was coming over to me; like a magnet it was drawn to me. Just then, a huge dray came lumbering down the street pulled by four horses. I yelled at the dog to stop, but the dog came straight at me. When the dray hit, the dog died instantly.

"Right then, in that dreadful, holy moment, the world opened up and I knew everything in the universe. Time stood still. There was no sound. I thought I saw the dog's spirit fly up through a conduit to that place that I now know exists outside of this sphere. The vision closed up at once, but this glimpse of eternity, or whatever it was, changed me in an instant. I knew there was something more than this life. In this lightning flash, my family became my most precious belonging. I knew I was part of forever. I was filled up to bursting.

"I looked again at the poor, dead, beautiful creature and then saw two young boys running over to where it lay. What I heard and saw next broke my heart to pieces. They called out to their dog, sobbing its name. "Rusty, Rusty, oh poor, Rusty."

Now Pa's voice gets husky and his face scrunches up. Tears pour from his eyes. He brushes them aside and continues.

"These two small children tried to pick the dog up, one at the head, the other at the rear, but it was too heavy for them. When passers-by tried to help lift the dog, they cried, "Get away, he is our dog."

Finally, they took off their jackets, tied them together, and made a sling for the poor animal. The last I saw was them half carrying, half dragging their Rusty home."

He pauses, takes a deep shuddering breath, and then continues. "So … my Rusty, my son …" but I put my fingers over his mouth to stop him from saying the unnecessary words.

We sit … not hearing the children's shouts, the bird calls, the chatter of the zoo monkeys, not seeing the sunshine dappling through leaves, the ants busily hauling their oversize loads. We sit … side by side, just feeling, just sensing some kind of strange echo throbbing between us.

*Cobweb *Restaurant *Blanket *Car park *Mattress *Bridge

HOME FOR CHRISTMAS

Saliva drizzled from between his quivering, chapped lips. It froze in the evening air, making an icy cobweb on his whiskered chin. He wasn't aware that he hadn't eaten for over three days. A vague recollection like a tired firefly winked slowly off and on in his head: turkey – dinner – Mission – Christmas day – come.

His stomach rumbled loudly, hollowly, like an empty boxcar. Startled, he lurched around to see who had spoken to him.

"Beg pardon?" he croaked.

A woman walking behind him gave a wide berth as she quickly rushed by, shaking her head in disgust.

"What is this world coming to?" she muttered to herself.

The threadbare, grey blanket, which his sudden movement had dislodged from his shoulders, lay on the wet pavement of the darkening street. His big hands, the colour of smudge, plucked at the makeshift poncho as he bent to pick it up. Like a marionette, lopsided and unsteady, he struggled to coordinate the simple movements needed for this simple task. It proved too much for him. Finally, after one more attempt to retrieve the blanket, he lurched away, his torso dragging his legs behind him like an afterthought.

Mud-coloured running shoes encased his bare feet. Like huge gravy boats, they slopped along. Primrose-yellow plastic twine laced them to his feet. This spot of yellow was the only colour about him. The rest was grey … grey from the faded jean jacket to the jogging pants … grey.

He glanced once more at the abandoned grey blanket. It lay like an old stain on a grey mattress, permanent. It had already become part of the side-walk in the growing dusk.

The icy rain, which had been misting, turned to a freezing drizzle, and the man hunched his thin neck into the frayed collar of his jean jacket. He had only a little way to go.

He had almost covered the two long blocks from his cardboard hamlet under the bridge to the Men's Mission. He saw the neon cross, white and welcoming. He felt a little warm glow in his stomach, but as he neared the building, he saw other men leaving the brightly lit common room.

He tried to quicken his stumbling gait. At last, he reached the door and fumbled for the knob. Someone on the other side turned the knob and pulled open the door, dragging the man inside. He collided with a large, sad-faced woman. She was tired. She had been at it all day.

"Oh, it's you, Thomas. We are closing now. You missed our lovely Christmas Eve concert and luncheon," she admonished, shaking her finger at him.

"You will come for Christmas dinner tomorrow, now won't you?" she cajoled as she gently pushed Thomas to the door.

"Goodnight, Thomas. Merry Christmas. God bless you."

Thomas shivered, blinked his eyes in bewilderment a few times, and then shuffled off down the dark alley behind the Men's Mission. He headed for the little exclusive French restaurant just around the corner.

The restaurant too was closing, but Thomas took his customary position just a few steps from the door. He reached into the pocket of his baggy sweat pants and drew out a crumpled paper. On it was written" "Please help a man low on luck". Thomas was proud of the note his friend Joseph Eagle Feather had written for him by the light of the car park stairwell.

Loud, raucous laughter made him jump, and he dropped the paper. A woman and a man staggered out of the restaurant door, holding each other up, laughing. Thomas sidled up to the couple, his paper forgotten, and in a cracked, faltering voice said, "Uh, you got couple bucks … for uh, some supper?"

"What's he saying?" the woman screeched.

"He wants a handout. Poor bugger," said the man, and he reached into his pocket and drew out a bill. He handed it to Thomas.

"Thanks'm," mumbled Thomas as he grasped the bill in his stiff fingers.

"Good grief, Fred," the woman screamed. "That's a twenty!" She snatched the bill from Thomas's hand and turned to Fred.

"He won't buy food! He'll drink it away! He can work for a living just like the rest of us! Look at him, Fred. For crying out loud, he's younger than you."

She grabbed Fred's arm and screamed in Thomas's face, "Get the hell out of here!"

She steered Fred towards a cab that had just pulled up at the curb, under the streetlight. The front door of the passenger side opened and a young girl got out.

"Okay, thanks, Rick. See ya around," she called to the driver and slammed the door.

"Get in dammit, Fred. Get in! This place is crawling with riff-raff."

Fred awkwardly opened the back door and the couple flopped inside.

"What riff-raff," she said again. as if she liked the taste of the words on her flabby lips.

A huge man stepped from the shadows and spoke quietly to the girl. "How'd it go Angel?"

"Great, just great Malcolm." She handed him two bills folded up neatly.

Malcolm counted them, "Mm, pretty good, pretty good."

"And that's not all. Look! I even got a bonus." She took a twenty-six of whiskey from her enormous handbag.

Malcolm took the whiskey in one big hand and drew her to him with the other. Out of the corner of his eye, he saw Thomas watching from the edge of the building. Malcolm let go of Angel and walked over to Thomas. He handed him the bottle of whiskey and thumped him on the back.

"Here man, not everyone's as miserable as those two tight-asses. Have a good one!"

Thomas clutched the bottle with both trembling hands. His vacant, slate-coloured eyes gave a brief flicker. A nod was all he could muster.

A drop of rain slid down his whiskered cheek as he turned towards the dark alley and home.

At the end of the alley, before Thomas could cross the street for the bridge, he heard someone say, "Hey Thomas, how's it going?"

Two policemen stood before Thomas blocking his way.

Thomas grunted, "Jest goin home."

He made a detour around the police officers and headed for the bridge.

The same two policemen found Thomas on Christmas morning under the bridge in his cardboard shanty.

"Looks like he died during the night. It was damn cold last night. Poor fella," one officer said."

The other officer replied, "Yeah, guess he really made it home this time."

PART FOUR
{'TIS}

'TIS

And so it is… and was…
And will forever be…
Life's canvas reflects
Back to self…
The who and what
We see.

EPILOGUE

Jake and Elsa Flowers became fast friends over the next few years. Jake got hitched last year, with the proviso in the solemn marriage troth that he was all his bride's, but for two hours every Sunday afternoon.

Last month, Jake became the father of a baby boy. He named him Aaron, the name of Maxine Lewis's ingenious, mindfully tender son.